Nightcrawler

Nightcrawler

John Reinhard Dizon

Published 2015 by Creativia
Book design by Creativia (www.creativia.org)
Cover Design by Cover Mint

Chapter One

"Bless me father, for I have sinned. It has been a couple of weeks since my last confession."

"There is only one Heavenly Father, and He alone forgives sins."

"I'm sorry, Pastor. Old habits die hard."

"Always good to see you, Bree. Have a seat."

Sabrina Brooks had been on a spiritual quest since the death of her father. He had left her as the sole heir of Brooks Chemical Company, and suddenly she had come crashing back to reality from a lifetime world of fantasy. She had been a spoiled child who grew up to be a party brat, only the death of her mother four years ago sobered her enough to earn her degree in chemistry at New York University. She was reluctantly stepping into the breach as her father's successor, but she needed answers to rest her troubled soul. She had finally come to the Force of God Christian Church on the Bowery, and Matt Mitchell was helping her find them.

Mitchell had opened the storefront church a year ago on a wing and a prayer, and Bree came at a time when the situation was just beginning to stabilize. People in the community sought stability in the Great Recession, and he had enough tithe-paying regulars to keep his doors open for believers in Truth. Bree came twice a month, and her donations were large enough to double the Church's income. She came by during the week now and again for counseling, and the pastor was always glad to oblige.

"I think I'm going to have to go back out," she said softly as they sat in the back office of the small but cozy meeting place.

"Why?"

"Have you seen the papers?"

The Pastor, a man in his fifties with receding gray hair and wire-rimmed glassed, looked down at the desk where Bree sat before him before answering.

"You know they've got Homeland Security, the FBI, and probably the military in on this," he said gently. "Do you really feel like they're in such need of help?"

"It's not about me. It's about the contract my father's company had with the military. These people are threatening the city with a chemical weapon. I can't help but think if there's a way to infiltrate the group by offering them technology in exchange for information, I might be able to save lives."

"Sabrina, we've discussed this situation before, and I don't think I've got any more suggestions or answers for you," he said resignedly. "I know your reasoning and your motivation, and you agreed that you found closure by apprehending those drug dealers a couple of months ago. Now we know that the Lord has a purpose for everyone in this life, and you may well have served one by doing what you did. At this point in time, you're being a great help to this ministry, this congregation and this community. I'm not sure you realize what a loss it would be to us if anything were to happen to you."

"I guess I'm weighing the benefits to the community as opposed to the benefits of the entire city."

"You've already made your mind up. You weren't expecting me to talk you out of it, I hope."

"I think I just wanted your blessing."

"I can't condone what you're doing, and I can't ask God to bless what you do."

"Can't you just bless me?" she asked plaintively.

"Of course I will. Let's pray together."

She had been on a path of self-discovery ever since her mother died. She thought of it as a time of self-enlightenment, though her father often thought of it as a path to self-destruction. She enrolled at New York University in pursuit of her degree in chemistry to follow in her father's footsteps. After her second year, she left for the John Jay College of Criminal Justice in pursuit of a career in law enforcement. In retrospect, she saw it as an act of rebellion in rejecting her father's legacy as heiress of BCC. Yet he would not coerce her into a career in chemistry, and she went on her way until she nearly burned her bridges behind her.

She did her best to earn the title of John Jay's Party Queen, carousing with her after-school clique until she began to realize that the scholars had dropped out of the gang and were being replaced by the short-termers. Her grades began plummeting from her 4.0 in NYU to a 2.0 at Jon Jay. She began skipping classes until she was on the verge of being dropped from half of them. She stopped discussing school with her Dad, and the time came when they had almost nothing in common to discuss. It was six months ago when he died of an aneurism, but those who knew him said he died of a broken heart.

One of those who believed so was his partner, Jon Aeppli. He was Vern Brooks' teacher and mentor at NYU, and when her Dad graduated and invested his inheritance in BCC, he made Aeppli an offer he could not refuse. Together they began working on projects they had long discussed at NYU, and when some of them garnered the interest of major American chemical corporations, the new company never looked back. Her Dad's death was a terrible blow to Aeppli, and it took a lot for him to come to the table with Sabrina and discuss a possible future.

They met at Keene's Steakhouse on West 36th Street near Madison Square Garden a week after the funeral. It was not lost on Aeppli that it was one of the places the Brookses would visit on Sabrina's birthdays. She had been left with a trust fund in her mother's will, and she would pick up $2,000 per month until her death. It was enough to pick up the tab, though Aeppli insisted on ordering one of the lowest-priced items on the menu.

"I thought you wanted to discuss either liquidating the company or buying me out," Aeppli seemed nettled after Sabrina went into her sales pitch.

"No, sir, I have put a great deal of thought into this. My father's life focus was on this company. This was his dream. I can't just sell it off and let it disappear."

"Let's not do this, Sabrina," Aeppli shook his head ruefully. "Let the company go with dignity. Your father would have wanted it that way."

"He would've wanted us to keep it going, Mr. Aeppli."

"Don't you think it's a little late for that?"

"What do you mean?"

"I'm sorry, Sabrina," Aeppli put down his napkin as if finished with the meal he had been picking at. "I told you, I don't want to do this. It's not going to change anything."

"Look, I came here to talk. I came here to keep my father's business alive, and you're the only one who can help me do it. Everybody knows that you and my Dad were the ones who made the Company tick. I can't expect any of the engineers to step into the shoes of either one of you. Mr. Aeppli, if it's about money…"

"Don't insult me, and don't insult your father's memory. If you made this decision four years ago, maybe things would have been different."

"Good," she rested her elbows on the table. "Let's talk. Okay, I was a stupid kid who made a lot of stupid mistakes back then. When my mother died, I thought my world had collapsed around me. I resented my father because I felt like still having me wasn't good enough for him. I know that was selfish and wrong but I can't change the past. I dropped out of NYU and went to Jon Jay not just to tick him off, but because I wanted something for myself. I thought being a cop might've been a way to change the world, and not just see myself as some spoiled little rich girl."

"Sabrina, you don't have to—"

"No, you let me finish," she wiped tears from her eyes, smearing her mascara. "The partying was psychological, like a self-fulfilling prophecy. I knew I was going to screw everything up, so I used the partying as an excuse. I knew it was hurting my father and I tried to stop but I'd just fallen too far. It's not like I wanted him to die, Mr. Aeppli—"

"Jon," he said softly.

"Jon," she managed a smile. "I thought he was going to live forever. I thought he was going to be there when I found the right guy and got married and had kids. If I could do it all over again, you know what I'd do. It's not too late, I can go back to school, I can get my degree and keep this Company going. But I can't do it without you, Jon. You know if my father were here he'd want you to give me just one chance. Please."

"Chemistry was never just a science for us, Sabrina. It was an art form. We always saw ourselves as master chefs. Sometimes we were like short-order cooks. We could throw a formula together in minutes. We used to test each other, make up formulas and ask each other if it would explode, turn into something else or just disintegrate. We liked what we did, and if you don't enjoy it like that then it's not for you."

"You can give that to me. You gave it to my Dad, you can give it to me."

"He already had it when I taught the first class I ever had him in," Aeppli was wistful. "He thought chemistry was fascinating. He would stay after class and ask questions, and he would be in the library after school and read about it. He didn't just study it, he read it like literature. I thought I was the only one in the world who felt that way about it until I met him. He would stop by the faculty lounge a couple of times a week to visit, all the way up until he graduated. He told me what he had planned, but I didn't really believe it, not even when he came to me with an offer to double my University salary and match my pension if I came in with him. One day I woke up and realized that it wasn't a dream, and it really happened. Even then, it was still like a dream until about two weeks ago."

"Give me a chance, Jon. Please."

"Okay, kid," he relented. "We'll meet in your Dad's office Monday and take a walk around the place, see what we got left."

She had not entirely given up on her dream of law enforcement either. She loved the camaraderie, the training, and the feeling that she was going to be saving lives and helping others. She was a big strong girl at 5'9" and 140 pounds, and loved hearing guys talk about her looks behind her back. She had long auburn hair, emerald eyes, and an hourglass figure highlighted by a generous bosom and perfectly chiseled legs. She had unusual tendon strength for a woman and had met very few men her size who could beat her no holds barred. She secretly dreamed of opening up a private investigation company one day but would not say a word of it to Jon Aeppli.

In looking back, she chalked it to her willful stubbornness, seeing it as something that everyone would have said she could not do. Though she knew she would lose Jon Aeppli forever if she even mentioned Jon Jay, she began keeping tabs on the rising crime rates and statistics in NYC. She started researching neighborhood crime watch groups, volunteer patrol clubs, and eventually vigilantism. She knew that with the right equipment, a trained, dedicated person could cruise around at night and be ready to lend a hand to those in need. She dwelled on it until it became an obsession, and eventually she knew she would have to give it a try.

The most important thing was to disguise the fact she was a woman. If she went up against a man, chances were they would fight to the finish rather than getting taken down by a girl. She decided on wearing a balaclava, a ninja uniform and SWAT gear. It would be a perfect combination of loose clothing and solid armor that would give her a unisex look. She would also carry standard SWAT equipment, only she would not pack a firearm. She would not take a life to save a life, and would instead explore other ways to incapacitate a perpetrator.

That was when she was hit with a bolt of inspiration. It would make all the sense in the world for her to develop non-lethal or non-crippling chemical weapons that she might eventually be able to offer to law enforcement agencies through BCC. It would also help her avoid physical combat against male attackers. Plus it would force her to spend more time researching in the lab, which could not hurt one bit.

She tried to think of a name for her alter ego in case she was ever forced to defend herself in the media. Undoubtedly her campaign would cause controversy, and if the socialist groups that controlled NYC turned against her, she would have to speak her peace or be branded as a criminal. She tried to think of something mysterious, something icky and unladylike, and eventually she thought of a Nightcrawler. It was the ugliest thing her father ever put on his fishing hook, and the name was perfect for what she planned to do.

She began ordering her equipment on the Internet little by little so as not to arouse suspicion. She also traveled around the City, far away from the family mansion on Staten Island, picking up items here and there. She continued to pay her dues at the YMCA and work out with her ex-classmates from Jon Jay whenever they stopped by. Only her sparring matches had gotten too intense, and finally a club manager called her aside and told her flatly that she needed to join a martial arts club instead of practicing at the facility.

Her last rollaround was with Hoyt Wexford, one of the 4.0 students who went on to the police academy. They had remained good friends, and Hoyt agreed to come in and work with her on Mondays. Even though he was six feet tall and 185 pounds, he had to turn it on to stay on top of her. It was their last sparring match that led to the manager prohibiting her from rolling around at the gym.

"Ow!" she yelled out when Hoyt slapped an arm bar on her and made her tap out. "You hurt me, you big dummy!"

"Well, that's it for me," he rolled off the mat and picked up his towel, wiping the sweat from his black mane and his ruggedly handsome face. "You're gonna have to find someone else to beat on."

"Oh, come on, Hoyt!" she said in disbelief. "You can't leave me hanging like that!"

"You're too much, Bree," he insisted. "I can't keep you off me without turning on the gas, and that's the truth of it. Look, for your own sake, you need to focus on other areas of martial arts, like forms and techniques. You're at a plateau right now, and the only place you can go is against people bigger than you, or professionals. You're liable to get yourself hurt, and for what? Let it go, Bree. Take it from a friend."

"Well, can't you still work out with me? Forms and techniques?"

"Yeah, sure," his blue eyes shone. "Same time Monday."

"You got a date," she got up and patted his back on the way to the showers.

"Say, Ms. Brooks," the gym manager came up to her. "Can I have a word?"

It was a week later when the elderly woman made her way home from church on a particularly windy night. Lorraine Hinton was a widow of twenty years, the septuagenarian devoting her remaining years to charity work in the community. She crossed 137th Street warily, looking both ways, the gang known by that name considering it a no man's land that none dared trespass at night. She had to cross the street to get home, though it was after nine and even the cops didn't come around here that late. East Harlem was the kind of place where you stayed home after dark with your doors locked.

Lorraine crossed the street and headed down Lenox Avenue when she detected movement in a doorway slightly behind her to her left. She drew her light jacket up tightly around her, tucking her purse in both arms under her bosom to hide it from view as best she could. Her wrinkled ebony hands tightened around it, though she only had her WIC card and five dollars with her. Yet she knew that these predators could care less, and would rob and beat a person out of sheer cruelty.

"Hey, Grandma," one of the gangsters called out to her as he walked behind her. Three of his fellows also loomed up from the darkness as they all began stalking her. "You got change for a dollar? I need some change so's I can get on the bus."

She picked up her pace, moving as fast as her spindly legs would take her without breaking into a run. Two of her friends had been mugged over the past six months, and one of the women had been beaten so severely she had been blinded for life.

"Hey old woman, you keep running like that and you gonna get hurt!" one gangster cackled. They watched with amusement as a late-model car cruised up to the curb alongside her, and Lorraine dodged away from it as she stumbled and ran.

"Oh, Lord Jesus, help me!" she cried out in terror as the gangsters trotted up to her, the car door opening as the driver rushed out to intercept her.

"Nobody gonna help you, you old witch," one of the gangsters cackled.

"Wanna bet?" the driver of the car turned to face them.

"Who the hell are you?" they demanded.

"You don't want to know."

Two of the gangsters whipped out switchblades, the eight-inch metal blades shooting out as the other two men began circling the dark figure and the cowering woman. The black-clad figure threw open its cloak and produced a strange-looking device that looked like a miniature leaf-blower. The gangsters hesitated for one moment, which was long enough for the figure to take aim and fire at the hoodlums to the right. The device belched out a thick cloud appearing as pancake mix, which completely engulfed the two muggers. They froze dead in their tracks, unable to see or breathe as their arms seemed unable to reach their faces. The figure pointed the device at the other two robbers, who turned and ran for their lives.

"Where do you live?" the figure asked Lorraine.

"Right up the street a ways," she managed, still recovering from her fright.

"C'mon, I'll give you a lift," the figure opened the passenger door, shoving one of the petrified muggers to the ground.

The elderly woman slipped into the black Porsche as the figure closed the door behind her. The driver gunned the engine as the car burned rubber, leaving a cloud of smoke and the beginning of an urban legend in its wake.

Chapter Two

About a month after Jon Aeppli had his meeting with Sabrina Brooks, he agreed to stay on as President of the company. Sabrina took over as Chief Executive Officer, cramming in as much information as she could about BCC in the process. Aeppli maintained the day-to-day supervision of the facility while Sabrina studied job proposals and reviewed upcoming projects in determining the future direction of BCC. It all seemed to be running smoothly, but there were some things that she did not know about the Company that her father had never mentioned.

Vern Brooks had been romancing people at the Pentagon, and had gotten the phone numbers of research bases in New Mexico where specialized chemical experiments were being conducted. The Government was always looking for ways to save money in these days of economic turmoil, so the offer of a low price bid was always of interest. Jon had accompanied Vern to Alamogordo, and they spoke to a number of high-ranking officers and scientists concerning a number of projects under consideration. To their surprise and delight, they were granted a contract with the Department of Defense developing antidotes for toxic gases.

Sabrina began accessing the account database in order to pick up where her father left off. To her dismay, she found that most of the research was being conducted exclusively by Jon Aeppli. He laid off most of the pick-and-shovel experiments with the BCC research team, compiling their findings into the larger account files and folders. She found that the research was focused on four main categories: blister, nerve, blood and choking agents. She decided that she would concentrate on modifying the chemicals for her own use, altering their qualities so that they were neither long-lasting nor injurious.

She began working on nettle and incapacitating agents, as these were areas not included in BCC's research. In doing so, she created a sub-folder in the main database for her own convenience. She had not heard anything from Aeppli as to the status of the Government projects, and assumed that they had been placed on the back burner. She also saw that the only ones who had access to the account database, known as the Black File, was her father, Aeppli, and the vice-presidents of BCC. Ryan Hoffman was the VP of the Research team, and Rick Alfonso was the VP in Development. It appeared that Hoffman and Alfonso's access was restricted to uploading, and were not able to view files without her father or Aeppli's permission.

She was in the private lab in the executive suite one night when she heard footsteps outside. She had been working by lamplight and took off her gold-rimmed glasses to see who had come by at such a late hour. She was surprised to see Jon Aeppli come through the door.

"Hi, Jon," she was pleasant. "You're up late."

"I see you've been burning the candlelight kinda late yourself," he sauntered over, pulling up a bench alongside the lab table upon which sat a large variety of equipment. "You certainly have exceeded expectations around here. Ryan and Rick have been telling me about how you've been coming around and learning about the day-to-day operations. They also mentioned about how you expedited a couple of orders that had caused some delays out on the floor. All in all, I think everyone's excited about your being here."

"Why, thank you," she simpered. "I was hoping I could make a positive contribution here while I'm getting up to speed."

"I just wanted to touch bases with you on a couple of things," Aeppli said quietly, the gray-haired man's brows knitted with concern. "I guess you know how the computer system's set up. Your Dad and I fixed it so it kept a log of who accessed what at whatever time so we could make sure we weren't duplicating work or stepping on each others' toes, so to speak."

"I noticed that right away. I'm sure that is very cost efficient."

"Well, the thing is, I saw you accessing the Black File a number of times over the past few weeks. I also saw you added a sub-folder. I took the liberty of checking out what you were working on. I just had a few questions."

"Why, sure. We're a team, we're partners, aren't we?"

"Since you've taken your father's place and I'm still here, that would be a reasonable assumption," he smiled wryly. "Did you know we put the project on hold due to budget cuts at the Pentagon?"

"Well, no, not really," she replied. "I've kinda been picking and pulling, snooping around, trying to get a handle on things. I guess I found that project pretty interesting."

"You certainly have. Did you know you were going to need a license for processing fentanyl to develop the methyl fentanyl you were looking at?"

"Well, I—uh—"

"Sabrina, I wasn't born yesterday," he said gently. "I know you haven't been able to let go of that law enforcement dream of yours. Is someone you know having you look into incapacitating agents for them?"

"Gosh, John, I—"

"One of us is going to have to give it to the other straight up, so I guess I might as well start," Aeppli was mildly exasperated. "There were some drug dealers who were taken to Bellevue about a week ago. They got hit with an anticholinergic compound and were defecating all over themselves. The doctors got suspicious of the nature of the powder the bad guys came in contact with and called the police, who notified Homeland Security. They started calling around and talked to me for about a half hour, especially after they learned about the Black File."

"That was something else I was looking at, that wasn't the Kolokol you and Dad were working on."

"I know that. You were working with something that looked a lot like Agent 15."

"I'd been doing some research, and thought that I might be able to expand upon the database somewhat—"

"What you're doing is dangerous, and could even get our license pulled," Aeppli admonished her. "Now I'd really like to know who's interested in this, and why."

"It's someone calling themselves the Nightcrawler," she said hesitantly. "It's like the friend of a friend. There's this area up in East Harlem where the cops don't patrol at night, and they've been targeting women, children and the elderly. They've been zeroing in on church groups that get together on weeknights. About a month ago they nearly beat an elderly woman to death for her purse. The Nightcrawler's trying to make them think twice about it."

"Why not just form a neighborhood patrol? Does this fellow really think the only solution is attacking the muggers with chemical weapons?"

"The gangs up there all carry guns and knives," she insisted. "I don't see the difference."

"That's because you're not seeing the big picture. If anyone ever traced any of those weapons to this facility, I would be legally liable as President of the Company. I've got a wife, and two grandchildren I'd like to help put through college. If we ever got sued it would destroy my life."

"I'm just doing the research," she lied. "I'm passing along the formulas."

"They could even come back at you with that if anyone were to be disabled or killed," he sighed. "You're on thin ice with this, kid."

"The Nightcrawler may have saved that old lady's life," Sabrina was adamant.

"What old lady?"

"The one they attacked to get themselves gassed," she insisted.

"Okay, I'll go along with it for now," he relented. "Just keep me in the loop, let me take a look at those formulas before they go out the door. There's a big legal difference and a slight chemical difference between incapacitating gas and poison gas."

"Gotcha, Jon. Thanks."

"Don't thank me just yet. If anyone gets hurt or the police start investigating us, this project of yours is dead in the water."

"I'll have them tell the Nightcrawler to be careful," she reassured him.

It was a couple of nights later when Ryan Hoffman was called to a meeting that he would rather have missed. He had been getting text messages on his cell phone that had been very disturbing, followed by automated voicemails threatening him with dire consequences if he did not return the call. He finally reached someone at an unlisted number who gave him directions to the rendezvous point, the Trinity Place Bar and Restaurant on Broadway and Cedar in the Wall Street area. The raucous atmosphere allowed for a confidential conversation as it was almost impossible to hear someone over a couple of feet away.

Hoffman made his way to a rear table in a far corner where the two women in black awaited. They were both tall, powerfully built women with visible tattoos on their necks and bosoms, their hair worn in Rastafarian-type braids though both were Caucasian.

"Your whole life story's in this envelope," the brunette shoved the parcel across the table to him. "Born in Brooklyn, raised on Long Island. You got your chemistry degree at LIU and hooked up with Vernon Brooks and Rick Alfonso at the Brooks Chemistry Company. You've got a wife and kids on the Island, and you're involved in a number of philanthropic groups and organizations. I'll bet it gets you some pretty nice tax writeoffs."

"So what's your point?" Hoffman insisted. He was a tall, dark-haired man with handsome features accentuated by blue eyes and a pencil-thin mustache.

"Our point is the best man at your wedding, Rick Alfonso," the blonde snapped at him. "You two have been at it for the past ten years, and hiding it pretty good, I might add. Our people hadn't figured it out until we started investigating the people in the Gotham AIDS Fund recently. Why would a good-looking guy with your kind of money, married with five kids, be throwing big bucks into an AIDS foundation for? We put a tail on you just for the hell of it, and sure enough. You and Rick don't work late by yourselves all the time just because you like to play with test tubes."

"What do you think you're trying to do here?" Ryan demanded. "Are you trying to infringe on my gay rights? You know all the new laws that have been passed. I'll have you both charged with a Federal offense! Blackmailing a gay person can get you twenty years in prison!"

"Look, we've been together for ten years ourselves, so you're barking up the wrong tree," the brunette smirked. "Besides, getting busted for civil rights violations is the least of our worries. We've got bigger fish frying, and you're gonna help."

"You two are out of your minds! You think you can just walk into my life—!"

"We know you're one of the three treasurers holding the account codes to the AIDS fund," the blonde stared at him. "We need those codes so we can launder a large sum through the account in the next few days. It's going to be a rapid deposit and an immediate withdrawal. It'll go in and out so fast the authorities won't be able to prove whether it was an accidental transaction until it's too late."

"You've got to be kidding!" Ryan exclaimed. "All three of us are immediately alerted by the bank whenever a transaction over $100 is processed on the account! You may be able to keep me quiet, but if either of my associates see your dirty money go through, they'll put a block on the account until the other two of us are contacted!"

"We'll take care of them when the time comes," the brunette assured him. "Here's our e-mail address. You have six hours to send us your access codes, passwords, and any other information we need to manipulate the account. It's six PM now, you have until midnight. If you don't help us out, we'll have documented proof of your relationship mailed to your wife, the administrative staff at Brooks Chemical, as well as Rick Alfonso's family and every gay-bashing right-wing organization in New York. After it's over, you'll have plenty of proof that you were blackmailed into helping us."

"Don't let a sixty-second transaction cost you your entire life," the blonde exhorted him as the two women got up and walked out of the restaurant. "Think of your wife and kids, and how you wouldn't want them to think of you if you don't help us out!"

Ryan Hoffman stared at the tabletop for a long, long time before he dissolved into tears.

Sabrina was at the office the next morning sorting out a pile of paperwork that seemed to multiply quicker than she could cut through it. She had been calling Jon, Ryan and Rick constantly throughout the day for advice for the first few weeks after she got there, but was finally figuring things out on her own and taking the initiative whenever she could. She was starting to see one particularly disturbing trend and called the executive sales manager, Chris Assante, in for a chat.

"Well, to be frank, Miss Brooks—", Chris spoke with a gay accent, crossing his legs with a feminine flair as he sat across from Sabrina at her father's large mahogany desk.

"Sabrina," she insisted with a friendly smile.

"Sabrina, I'm sorry," he corrected himself. "Since your father's passing, it seems like many of the companies we've been negotiating with seem to be reluctant to make a commitment. Many of them seem to anticipate internal problems with the transition and adjustment process."

"That's ridiculous," she scowled. "Jon, Ryan and Rick are still running the show. I'm just sitting up here directing traffic, you've been around enough to know that."

"It's not just that," he replied. "Now, this is just between you and me, but I'm starting to get the impression that a lot of people are uneasy over the prospect of having a woman as CEO of their research company. You know what kind of man your father was, with his personality and leadership. They just can't see a woman bringing that to the table, even if you are his daughter."

"They don't even know me, they don't know anything about me!" she was adamant. "Just because I'm a woman, they think I can't run this company? Why don't you set up some follow-up sales calls and I'll go out with you?"

"Well, that's part of what I wanted to talk with you about, Sabrina," Chris was hesitant. "I'm not sure how much longer I'm going to be staying on."

"Now what's this about?" she was taken aback. "You've been with us for over ten years."

"My partner's been offered a position with a major land developer in Florida near Orlando. They offered him a ten thousand dollar annual increase in salary. Plus we're looking at property out there. He's always wanted to live near Orlando, you know, the Disney World thing. It's just a change in lifestyle, it has nothing to do with what's happening here."

"Well, it sure is coming at a heck of a time for us," she exhaled tautly. "When are you planning on leaving?"

"I was really thinking about the end of next month. I'd be more than happy and work with Micah Malloy and get him up to speed to replace me, that is, if you don't have anyone else in mind. I'd also love to set up some power lunches and get you out to meet with some of those old fogeys. In my opinion, I think you'll do a great job, and I'm going to do my best to let everyone else know it."

"I'll be doing my best to make sure you don't go to Florida feeling like you left a train wreck behind you," she said sweetly.

She was about to wrap it up at the office when she got a call on her cell phone from Hoyt Wexford. Her heart jumped for joy as it was the bright spot in a cloudy day thus far. Jon Aeppli seemed a bit moody, undoubtedly over the discussion they had the other night. Ryan Hoffman also seemed down in the dumps, and that wasn't making his close friend Rick Alfonso very happy.

"Hoyt! How are you!"

"Great. I just thought I'd touch bases, see what your schedule looked like this week."

"I'd love to go down and meet you tomorrow night," she replied happily. "It's been kinda stressful around here, and I could really afford to let off some steam."

"Sounds like a plan. How're things going at the corporate office? I'll bet it's really exciting, being the new CEO of the family company."

"I'll tell you, Hoyt, it's kinda like jumping out of an airplane wondering if your parachute's gonna work," she managed a laugh, gazing out the window overlooking the East River from the scenic view along the Staten Island shore.

"Say, big guy, I gotta go. I was just getting ready to close it down for the evening. Six o'clock at the YMCA tomorrow?"

"You got it. Just be gentle with me, okay?"

"Not to worry. The gym manager pulled me over after our last workout. No more women rolling around in the YMCA."

"Good. I've got some forms and technique drills that resemble insanity workouts. See you tomorrow, green eyes."

"Bye."

All of a sudden, Hoyt Wexford had her walking on air.

Chapter Three

Sabrina met Hoyt at the YMCA the next evening and it was one of the most enjoyable times she had in a long while. They worked out for about an hour, and Hoyt was somewhat surprised that she was able to keep the pace with him. She suspected that he was intensifying the routine to assert himself, but when he realized he wasn't going to wear her out, he settled into a more rhythmic flow. She was concerned that he might feel threatened by her, especially since he was a cop living in an alpha male environment. Yet she sensed a soft and caring side to him, and she hoped to tap into that if anything meaningful developed between them.

"Gee, you're in great shape," she smiled as she toweled herself off after the workout. "I could barely keep up."

"Don't blow smoke up my nose," he scoffed. "You're like a cardiovascular machine. I'd hate to see you on a track, you'd be making Olympic sprinters cry. Tell you what, why don't we go get something to eat so I can load you up on some carbs? Maybe next time I'd have a better chance keeping up with you."

He met her out in the lobby and was caught off guard as she emerged from the women's locker room. She had her hair pinned up, wearing a dark blue power suit which accentuated her lovely legs, with matching high heels, Gucci purse and a tasteful pearl necklace. It was a far cry from how she dressed as a student at John Jay, and he almost felt self-conscious in his NYPD baseball jacket and hangout clothes.

"Geez, lady, I can't imagine what you look like when you get dressed to go out," Hoyt managed a laugh.

"Well, I'll take that as a compliment," she arched an eyebrow. "You think we can go over to my car so I can drop off this gym bag?"

He walked her to the nearby parking garage, admiring the Mercedes-Benz she inherited from her father. They next headed over to the Caracas Arepa Bar on East 7th Street where they opted for the La Vegetariana platter on the Curiaras menu. She found the traditional Spanish décor pleasing and the local ambiance cozy with the college crowd and local professionals that frequented the restaurant.

"So how's that promotion looking for you?" she asked as she savored a bite of her Leek Jardinera *arepa*. She walked around hungry most of the time and depended on her veggie snack bag, vitamins and bottled water to get her through each day. "You haven't said much about it."

"Well, I'm not sure how it's gonna go down," he replied as he took a sip of his iced tea. "There's probably a couple hundred guys competing for five open slots. Everybody wants to be on the SWAT team. It's some fierce competition, with all the guys having returned from Iraq and Afghanistan, plus the guys messing with the mixed martial arts. I'm gonna give it my best shot and hope for a miracle or two."

"Don't think like that," she insisted. "It can't be all about brute force. Guys who get picked for special units have to be intelligent as well. They've got to be able to think on their feet, they just can't run out there like GI Joe and blow up everything in sight. Look at those fellows who took out Bin Laden. Pulling the trigger must've been the easy part."

"You're right about that," he smiled. "Maybe you'll be my lucky charm. With a little brains and a lotta luck, anything can happen."

"Good," her eyes sparkled. "I'll give you a picture of me you can carry around like a rabbit's foot."

"You know, I'd really like that."

They finished their meal and he walked her back to her car. Most of the NYU students had returned to campus for their night classes, and the lot was fairly deserted.

"So, same place next time?" he sounded hopeful as she cut off the alarm and popped the car door.

"Well, uh, I was wondering," she was hesitant. "You know, there's this church I go to down on the Bowery, it's about ten minutes from here. They have these lunch fellowships once a month, and they've been inviting me to go for a while now. I was wondering, if you weren't doing anything on Sunday morning, maybe I can meet you out there. The pastor has a great message and the people are friendly. We could go on over and have lunch with the brothers and sisters afterward if you'd like."

"Go to church?" he was surprised. "I don't know if they'd want me in there, I was raised Catholic. My folks are Irish all the way."

"They're non-denominational, that means anyone can come," she said cheerily. "I went through twelve years of parochial school myself."

"Okay, let me figure this out," he shook his head. "A beautiful ex-candidate for the police academy, running her own chemical company, and a churchgoer to boot. You're something else, Bree."

"Well, thanks," she blushed.

"I'll give you a buzz on your cell phone Saturday, okay?" he patted her shoulder, giving it an affectionate rub before he walked off.

"Sounds great. Be careful," she called to him, feeling her heart skip a beat as he headed off into the darkness.

The next morning, she arrived at the office and was surprised to see Ryan Hoffman waiting at the receptionist's desk for her. She normally got there an hour early to set a good example for the one hundred employees at the facility. Jon, Ryan and Rick usually arrived a half hour after she did. She felt her gut tighten as she fervently hoped that Ryan was not going to be the next one to announce his resignation.

"Good morning, Miss Brooks," he seemed ill-at-ease. "Can I have a word with you?"

"Why sure, Ryan. Try Sabrina," she smiled uncertainly. "C'mon in."

Ryan took a seat in front of her desk after closing the door behind him. He seemed under a lot of stress and appeared not to have gotten enough sleep.

"I know you went to John Jay for a while and probably made some connections with people in the police department," he began. "I was kind of wondering if you may have someone you could reach out to with a personal problem."

"Well, no one anywhere up the ladder, but the guy I'm going to church with carries a badge."

"Miss Brooks—Sabrina—I've got a problem," he said hoarsely.

She sat quietly as he told her all about the women who met with him at the Trinity Restaurant. She remained impassive, taking notes as he told her everything that had happened. After he finished, he appeared as if about to cry, and she realized she would have to earn his trust as the first step in resolving the problem.

"First off, I really don't think you're going to have to worry about your wife and kids," she said reassuringly. "I'd bet the deed to this place that your wife already knows. Females have this thing called intuition that they use a lot. I've been a female all my life, I should know."

They shared a laugh as Ryan wiped a tear from his eye.

"I'm pretty sure your kids know too. If they've accepted you all your life, they're not gonna stop any time soon. Now, I want you to go back to your desk and write down everything you can remember about the meeting with those two women. Tell me what they looked like, what they sounded like, anything I can use to see if these two have any priors. From what you're telling me, I'll bet you lunch at Mickey D's they do."

"Thank you, Sabrina," he managed. "Thank you so much."

"I wouldn't worry about this place either," she added. "We've got quite a few gay men working here, and I think they know too. You'll always have a job here."

He thanked her profusely as he returned to his office, leaving Sabrina wondering how she was going to deal with a problem like this without throwing Ryan Hoffman under a bus.

She got a call later in the day from one of the women at the church, which came as a surprise because no one had ever called from the congregation before. She was in the middle of reviewing Chris Assante's sales assessment and report sheets, trying to figure what would be her best strategy for damage control. She wasn't sure whether her best move would be to kiss the butts of some of her biggest clients and try to keep them in the fold, or take the gamble and reach out to the best prospects and see whether they could help take up the slack. Her gut feeling was to start with a clean slate, but she knew a major exodus of high-paying clients could prove disastrous.

"Miss Brooks?" she recognized the voice. "This is Audrey Smith from church. I really didn't want to bother you, but something's come up and I was just trying to reach out to as many people from the congregation that I could."

No, no bother at all," she took off her glasses and rubbed her eyes. "What's up?"

"I think you may have heard about the support group we were trying to organize for some of the at-risk teenagers in some of our families," Audrey replied. "It's just not happening quickly enough for some of them. I'm sure you've heard about the crack epidemic that's been plaguing our community. A lot of the young girls and unwed mothers are being victimized by drug addicts trying to get money to support their habits. Lots of these guys are resorting to violence, and it's getting completely out of control. Some of the girls are having to leave their homes and have no place to stay. We were thinking that maybe if we put our heads together, we can figure out a way to help some of them."

"All right, I'll be leaving here in an hour or so, I'm at the office right now. I can meet with you at the church about six-thirty."

She slumped back in her overstuffed swivel chair, kicking her stockinged heels against the carpet in exasperation. She had so much to do to keep the company afloat, she felt as if she was the one who was drowning. She had agreed to lend a hand with the outreach program at the church, but this was coming at an inopportune time. Yet she did not want to let the congregation down, and was starting to feel as if her obligation to the church was becoming the most important in her life. Her father's company was the most important thing in her world, but she knew her relationship to God was bigger than her world.

It was with that in mind that she drove down to the church, where Pastor Mitchell and twelve of the women of the church awaited. She found out that there were six young girls who were relatives of church members who were in desperate need of emergency shelter. The Pastor had arranged for lodging for three of them, and two would be allowed to spend the night here at the church with their infants. One of them was placed in lockdown by her crack addict boyfriend, and he was holding her incommunicado after severely beating her the night before.

"She refuses to press charges, and her six-year-old son is too afraid for her to say anything to the police or the social workers," the pastor explained. "The man of the house in belligerent and violent, and her aunt believes he's trying to get her to sign over her savings she's set aside to care for the boy. He sells their benefit cards and uses whatever's left of their welfare money on crack."

"Okay," Sabrina exhaled. "I'll go over with sister Rita and see if we can get him to let her have medical treatment."

"Please be careful," he insisted. "I'd go with you but the girls who are staying here are very afraid that the men may be coming after them over here. The police are being very cooperative but they don't have the resources to leave a patrol car out here."

Rita Hunt was a tall, attractive woman standing 5'6" and weighing 130, with shoulder length chestnut hair and a pretty Scottish face. She and Sabrina had chatted numerous times after services and hit it off well, though she was ten years older than Sabrina at thirty-four. She was unhappily married, had a daughter, and relied on God and the church as her place of refuge. The abused girl, Emma, was a great-niece who she had only seen a couple of times over the past five years. The family turned to Rita in desperation and she, in turn, turned to the church.

Hijo Shabazz had been in prison for over a dozen assaults and robberies, and was in and out of treatment for crack addiction. He met Emma in Alphabet City in the Bowery near Avenue A and East 7th Street, and moved in with her in exchange for free crack. Once he got her addicted, he began having sex with her and began presenting himself to neighbors as her boyfriend. Shabazz stood 6'3" and weighed 200 pounds, and had little problem physically controlling the 5'2", 110 pound girl. He ruled her three-year-old son Bobby with an iron hand, and beat Emma unmercifully when he did not get his way.

The women pulled up in Sabrina's black Porsche, which she alternated with her Dad's Mercedes Benz during the week for variety. They walked into the three-story brownstone and wrinkled their noses at the strong odor of urine and used diapers in the vestibule. The doorbell did not work and the front door was broken open, so they walked to the rear of the grungy hall and knocked on the door of apartment 1-B.

"Hello?" tiny Bobby appeared in the doorway.

"Hi, Bobby, I'm your Aunt Rita, remember me? Can I speak to your Mommy?"

"What the hell you opening that door for!" they heard a monstrous voice roar from inside. "Get your little butt back here!"

"But it's my Aunt Rita!" the little boy was frightened.

"I don't care if it's Barack Obama! Get your ass in here!"

At once the women were taken aback by the ferocious-looking black man appearing in the doorway, wearing a stained, sleeveless T-shirt over his tattooed body and cornrows in his hair. His eyes bulged with rage and his giant lips bared to reveal gold-capped teeth.

"What the hell you women want?" he demanded.

"I beg your pardon, sir," Rita was appalled. "I'm Emma Hunt's great-aunt. The family was notified after she was taken to the hospital the other day. Her mama lives in Kentucky, and they asked me to come out and make arrangements for her and the little boy to go down and visit until she gets to feeling better."

"She ain't going nowhere!" he snarled. "I takes care of her right here, and she be fine!"

"Sir, I'd like to speak with her and have her tell me it's fine with her."

"Look, she ain't feelin' well and she ain't takin' no visitors! Now get your white asses out my doorway and I'll have her call you."

"Sir, there is no reason to have an attitude towards me," Rita insisted, stepping towards the doorway. "I insist on seeing if my niece is okay!"

"And I told you she ain't seeing no one!" he feinted towards her, causing her to nearly stumble backwards.

"We can have someone else come by if you'd rather have a man-to-man talk," Sabrina said menacingly.

"I'm telling you for the last time, you better get your little white ass outta here," he stuck his finger in Sabrina's face. "You send some cracker out here and I'll rip his head off!"

"Fine," she said tautly. "You just wait right here."

"I think we'll have to let the authorities handle this," a tear trickled down Rita's cheek as they left the building.

"I don't," Sabrina was beside herself with indignation. "Rita, I want you to swear to me before God that you won't betray me if I take care of this for you."

"You do whatever you want to help that little girl in there," Rita insisted.

Sabrina popped the trunk and pulled her ninja jacket, her balaclava and her utility pouch out of her workout bag. Rita watched wide-eyed as Sabrina tossed her purse into the trunk after pocketing the car keys, then slamming it shut and storming back towards the building.

"What are you gonna do?" Rita stood flabbergasted.

"I'll be right back."

Hijo heard the hammering on the door and threw it open, both surprised and infuriated to see the dark figure in the doorway.

"What the hell you doing here, you runty little—!"

The ninja jacket had metal forearm guards sewn into both sleeves, and the figure sent one as a hammerblow across Hijo's face. He staggered backward as his nose was broken, and at once the figure threw a sandy-colored powder in his face. His throat was immediately clogged with mucus but he was unable to gag or spit because his face had frozen as if turned to stone. The figure then grabbed the edge of his hand and twisted it towards the ceiling, leading him by his locked arm into the kitchen. Bobby watched in awe as the figure produced a roll of duct tape and taped Hijo's wrist in the locked position to a radiator pipe in the corner.

"Wow," Bobby was amazed. "Are you Batman?"

"You just tell your Mom the police'll be here in ten minutes to take her to shelter," the figure spoke in an electronically-distorted voice through a device on the balaclava.

"Gee, you talk funny," Bobby said as the figure looked into the bedroom. Emma appeared to have been sedated, her bruised face angelic in repose.

"So do you," the figure teased him.

She was still psyched, and as an afterthought she fumbled beneath the ninja jacket and found lipstick in her suit pocket. She pulled off the cap and scrawled on the refrigerator door:

ZERO TOLERANCE ————- NIGHTCRAWLER

She regretted it almost as soon as she wrote it, but was not about to try and erase it with Rita waiting outside. She glared at Hijo as he remained bent over with his wrist tied at an excruciating angle up behind his back, foaming at the mouth.

"You walk funny too," Bobby giggled as the figure's hips swayed in leaving the apartment.

"What happened?" Rita stared as Sabrina hurried back to the Porsche, pulling off the ninja jacket. "Is everything okay?"

"Call the—" Sabrina said with a squawky voice, then yanked the balaclava and the voice distorter off her head impatiently. "Call the police and tell them to get her to the shelter. I'll get you back to the church so you can get everything set up."

"I owe you," Rita was misty eyed as they got in the car. "I don't know how to thank you."

"Don't thank me, praise the Lord," Sabrina smiled, trying to smooth her hair out. "You can buy me a cup of coffee sometime, and a chocolate donut."

Sabrina drove back out to Staten Island after dropping Rita off in front of the Force of God Christian Church, leaving it to her to explain everything to the Pastor. Undoubtedly the police would ask Rita what happened at the apartment, but her story was that the women had been threatened by Hijo and fled the premises before calling 911. They would be left with Bobby's tale about a ninja coming into the house and tying Hijo to the radiator before writing graffiti on the refrigerator.

She went back to the apartment to change into a T-shirt and jeans after taking a quick shower and grabbing a bag of rabbit food. She took the ten-minute drive to the BCC campus and headed inside to look over some contracts and proposals. She took the elevator to the second floor and was somewhat surprised to see Jon Aeppli's office light on in the darkened suite.

"Hey, Jon," Sabrina leaned into the doorway. "I hope your wife isn't blaming me for this."

"I really didn't try and give her much of an explanation," Jon's pale blue eyes bored into hers. "That friend of yours really made an impact tonight, didn't he?"

"Who was that, Hoyt?" she asked weakly, slipping into the armchair in front of Jon's desk.

"I take it you haven't seen the news or gotten on the Internet."

"Well, not really."

"That Nightcrawler friend of yours attacked a man in his own home with a chemical weapon a few hours ago," Jon was nettled. "The man happened to be a distant relative of the Mayor's partner. He's got the Mayor out for blood. The NYPD has an all-points alert out for the Nightcrawler. Your guy was crazy enough to leave a handwritten note on the victim's refrigerator."

"You mean the Mayor's a sissy?" Sabrina was wide-eyed.

"That's really not the issue here," Jon leaned over the desk towards her. "Besides, if you hadn't spent so much time partying over the last couple of years instead of watching the news, you would've known that. At any rate, the Mayor's partner says his nephew was gassed because he was a black man living with a white woman, and the assailant allegedly told him that when he attacked him. He even said the zero tolerance note was a warning to blacks who date white women."

"That lying dog!" she exploded. "He beat her so bad she was taken to the hospital the night before! It had nothing to do with race, it was a warning to guys who beat on women!"

"Now how would you know that?" Jon said gently.

At once the tension boiled over, and Sabrina cupped her forehead as she covered her eyes, weeping softly. Jon got up from his desk and walked around, patting her shoulder softly.

"It's okay, kid," he consoled her.

"It happened so fast, he made me so mad, and he was acting like he was going to hit my friend Rita," she sobbed as Jon handed her a handkerchief. "He was treating that little boy so mean, and I knew he had just put that poor girl in the hospital. I knew I should've never gone over there, but they didn't have anyone else and the Pastor couldn't go. I was just so upset."

"Bree, you're not telling me you're the Nightcrawler," Jon said in disbelief.

"I didn't say that," she sniffed halfheartedly.

"For crying out loud," Jon walked over to the plate glass window and stared out unseeingly at the river. "What on earth have you gotten yourself into?"

"I was just trying to make a difference, I wasn't trying to hurt anyone or get in trouble," she wailed. "I knew if I tried to get back into the Academy, you'd probably leave me. I just thought that with all this money, and the chemical weapons you and my Dad developed, maybe I could do something to help people. How could I have known this was going to happen?"

"Well, I can't walk away from you now," Jon shook his head as he turned to face her. "Now, you listen up, young lady. No more Nightcrawling for you, it's over. As your father's friend, I'm not gonna stand by and watch you get yourself killed. This all ends tonight, you understand?"

"Yes, sir," she wiped her eyes.

"We've got enough on our plate trying to keep our doors open without you going out and risking everything using chemical weapons on the street," he admonished her. "We'll just pretend this never happened, and when the Homeland Security people come back—which I know they will—I'll whitewash this as best I can. You just focus on being the CEO of this Company, and make sure you don't do anything to ruin your family name!"

"Okay, Jon," she smiled sweetly. "I promise."

She left the office shortly afterward, and returned home to spend an hour of quiet time with the Lord, asking Him to show her the right way.

She had no way of knowing that the powers of darkness were not about to let her walk away so quickly.

Chapter Four

"The days of discrimination against minority groups in New York City has come to an end!" Mayor John Jordan fumed as the crowded conference room at City Hall burst into applause. "This Administration will never tolerate hate crimes against any citizens in this City, and we will not abide by any acts of racial or gender discrimination! We are asking that this criminal calling himself the Nightcrawler turn himself in so that we can get him the kind of help and counseling he needs to live a productive life in rejoining our community. The kind of racial hatred he represents must be stopped at all costs, and we ask anyone who has any information about the hateful attack on Hijo Shabazz call 1-800-CRAWLER immediately."

"Man, what happened to you, brother, turning yourself out like that," UFC champion and ex-football player Lorenzo Jefferson sidled over to the Mayor's significant other, Mohammed Lincoln. Mohammed was also an NFL veteran who had supposedly come out of the closet last year.

"Brother, if all I got to do is take care of some dude for all this money and power, then I can just close my eyes when the lights go down and pretend I'm taking care of somebody else, you hear what I'm sayin'?" he said as they shared a hearty laugh.

On an upper floor, a tall, powerfully-built man in a dark blue designer suit walked into the Mayor's Office, smiling politely at the secretary.

"How can I help you?" he lisped.

"Perhaps you can," the blond, ruggedly handsome man smiled. "I'm a reporter with *New Socialist* magazine, and I had this all-access pass from last year. Can you see if this is still good?"

"I sure can, sweetie," he smiled pleasantly at the man. "Just one second."

The man pulled an unmarked legal-sized envelope from his inside jacket pocket and slipped it into the pile of letters in the IN box on the desk, then turned and walked out as he winked to the secretary.

"I think I gave you an expired card. Sorry."

"No problem. Have a great day," the secretary smiled, then sighed happily as he resumed his paperwork.

Dalibor Branko walked out of the office, smiling and shaking his head in disgust. He had been virulently homophobic since his teenage years as a volunteer in the Serbian Liberation Army. He had been on a personal crusade against Muslims, homosexuals and Communists, and rapidly rose through the ranks of the Army of the Serbian Republic as the Serbian War progressed through the 90's. After he fled Serbia to avoid prosecution for war crimes, he migrated to the USA and made connections with the Russian Mob in Brooklyn. He decided to start his own gang, and thought it was a masterful touch to recruit exclusively from the homosexual community.

He was known as the Grim Reaper in Bosnia and Kosovo for his willingness to execute Muslim captives, annihilating entire hamlets without hesitation. Upon arriving in America, he became known simply as the Reaper. He and his hand-picked LGBT (*lesbians, gays, bisexuals and transvestites) team had become specialists at murder, extortion, loan sharking and arson for the Russians. They saw so much money pass through their hands that Branko thought it idiotic to continue working under the sanction of others.

Mayor Jordan had held the press conference at ten AM that Saturday morning, and the unmarked letter was opened by his secretary and brought to his attention less than an hour later. The Mayor immediately contacted Police Commissioner John Martin, who in turn called Chief Joel Madden and Captain Ty Willard for an emergency session. Homeland Security and the FBI were also notified as to details of the mysterious letter.

"Gentlemen, it appears that we've got another wacko on the loose," the Commissioner brought the meeting at One Police Plaza to order. "Just a couple of hours ago, an unmarked letter was discovered at the Mayor's Office demanding the transfer of one million dollars to a bank account to be specified by a group claiming to be connected to Al Qaeda. This nut job is calling himself the Reaper, claiming he's the leader of a group known as the Octagon."

"Sounds like a bunch of UFC rejects, if you ask me," a cop called out, causing the room to echo with laughter.

"This sicko claims to have access to an anthrax bomb he is going to detonate at an undisclosed point along the East River," Chief Madden spoke up. "The White House has been notified, but as you know, this Administration refuses to negotiate with terrorists. At this point, we'll be looking at every known and suspected Al Qaeda sympathizer and Muslim militant activist group on record. We want everyone to scour their databases, squeeze every informer we've got on the field, and follow every lead that comes in to nip this thing in the bud. We don't need another Boston Massacre here in the City, people. We haven't leaked anything to the papers yet, so let's put these dirtbags away before this gets out of hand."

Just the night before, Hoyt Wexford and Sabrina Brooks had been socializing with a group of the officers who had been summoned to that meeting. They had convened at 310 Bowery, where more than a couple of franchises had tried and failed to make it in NYC's volatile economy. Sabrina knew most of the cops from the academy class that Hoyt had graduated from. They were happy to see her again and very glad that she was doing so well.

"Hey, Bree," one of the cops called as she returned to their joined tables from the restroom. "We just voted you as having the Best-Looking Feet in this place."

"Why, thanks, guys," she smiled, holding her leg up and wiggling her toes in her gold sandals.

"We were gonna vote you having the Best Butt, but some of the faeries around here might've insisted it should've gone to Hoyt," another cop joked. "We definitely didn't want to get accused of discrimination, so we let it go."

"What's this world come to?" a third cop bellowed in exasperation as a nearby table of gay men stared at them angrily. "How can anyone not appreciate the perfection of Bree's backside? Lady, I think you and me need to find ourselves a deserted island somewhere. This world is definitely screwed up."

"Not happening, I already got first prize," Hoyt waved him off. "You get to ride a fairy out to Fruitcake Island."

"Definitely screwed up," another cop sipped from a case of Bud bottles opened and unopened across the tables. "How do you figure that Nightcrawler guy, anyway? I talked to a couple of the guys who investigated the call at that apartment the other day. They said the note was written in lipstick on the wife-beater's ice box. Everybody out there said it looked more like he got what he deserved for putting that girl in the hospital. The Mayor's boyfriend was the one who played the race card."

As it turned out, the investigating cop who went out to the church after the incident only took Rita Hunt's name in his report. Sabrina was only mentioned as a 'second person' on the scene. The cop was more interested in learning the identity of the masked man who Hijo and little Bobby described, and Rita truthfully declared she never saw a man out there. Hijo wanted to blow it off because of what he had done to Emma, but when his uncle found out what happened, he would not let it go.

"I couldn't wrap my head around that chemical weapons angle," one cop admitted. "If he's got the kind of stuff they say he's got, then why isn't he committing an act of terrorism somewhere? They said they saw the same pattern with that attack up in East Harlem a few weeks ago. I'll betcha he's just a do-gooder hitting the dirtbags with some souped-up pepper spray."

"This whole country's gone paranoid since 9/11, and the Boston Massacre had made things worse," a cop scoffed. "Next thing you know, they'll ban the Fourth of July because of all the people carrying explosives."

"Here's to the Nightcrawler," another cop raised his bottle. "May all the wife-beating animals in this city get what they deserve!"

"Here's to Twinkletoes!" the first cop stood up in a toast to Sabrina. "May I get that deserted island vacation I deserve!"

"Yeah? Well, here's to Fruitcake Island," she retorted as they all howled with laughter.

Sabrina called Hoyt the following afternoon and was deeply disappointed when he told her he would not be able to meet her at church on Sunday morning.

"Gee, what's wrong?" she asked softly. "Was it something I said the other day?"

"Of course not," he chuckled in exasperation. "Everybody had a great time. The guys were all glad you see you again. A couple of them were kinda jealous that I was still getting to work out with you. It's just that something came up at work. They're putting a few of us on stand-by alert."

"Why, what's going on?"

"Well, it's sort of like that thing with the Special Forces and their top secret missions. I'd be letting you in on highly classified information. If you were to divulge any of the information I'd have to spank you."

"I suppose I'll have to take that risk, Hoyt," she got very quiet and serious sounding. "Now tell me!"

"There was a note that turned up at the Mayor's Office warning of a terrorist attack," he relented. "It's got everybody paranoid after the Boston Massacre. I think we're just going high-profile to send a message. They'll probably have us working overtime for the next couple of weeks, I guess. I'd be glad to take you out for dinner to make it up."

"Promise not to spank me?"

"Scout's honor."

"Let me know where and when."

She had called him from the office, and immediately stopped what she was doing to consider the situation. This had to be the gang that tried to blackmail Ryan Hoffman. She was very close to having ditched the whole Nightcrawler project, but her sense of responsibility was dumping it right back on the table. Undoubtedly they would be contacting him soon, and she realized she would have to work with him to make a connection with the terrorists.

"No, I haven't heard anything from them yet," Ryan admitted after Sabrina had called him into her office. It was a Saturday, but all the upper management personnel were putting in a couple of hours in an effort to accelerate some of their projects in stimulating cash flow. "Have you found out anything about those two people who met with me?"

"Not yet. Ryan, I was wondering if you knew anyone who works in upper management at the New York Telephone Company. I'm thinking we can do a trace on the numbers that try and make contact with the switch that controls the electronic transactions for the Fund."

"Well," he mused, "there was this one guy I dated back a few years ago before Rick and I began having our affair. He had a lot of top-level access, but I haven't spoken to him for quite a while. He's like me, he's still in the closet, he has a wife and two kids."

"Maybe that's how you'll be able to reach out to him," she pointed out. "If you tell him you've been blackmailed, he'll see how people like this can make anyone a victim unless gay people join together to defend themselves."

"Okay, I'll talk to him," Ryan said uneasily. "It's like I said, I haven't seen him for a couple of years. Plus I don't know if he's going to be worried that the gang might try and get revenge against him if they find out he's helped me."

"You've got to make him see that blackmailing gays is just another kind of terrorism," she insisted. "If you give in to them, it just inspires greater demands. If you hadn't come to me, they would've probably tried to make you a permanent part of their money-laundering network. Plus, if their scheme was discovered, they'd just cut you loose and leave you with the blame."

"All right, I'll call him," Ryan's voice was taut with fear.

"I'm going to be here for most of the afternoon," she assured him. "I'd be more than glad to go meet him. As a matter of fact, maybe you can set us up for Starbucks later on."

"Let me see what I can do."

She went back to reviewing her reports, trying to stay focused despite all the distractions spinning around her head. She was suddenly concerned about Hoyt and hoped he did not get thrown into a hot spot anywhere. She knew that the blackmailers who had contacted Ryan were probably planning on making their move soon. She was just as certain that it involved the terror threat that Hoyt told her about. She knew that this was getting too big for her, and she might have to get Jon involved lest she fumbled the ball and made strategic blunders that could never be undone.

The phone rang again, and she was nearly flustered by the caller ID but composed herself nonetheless.

"Bree? Hi, it's Rita."

"Hi, hon, how are you?"

"Oh, just fine. Say, the Pastor asked me to call to see if you might be available this evening for an hour or so. We've had something come up with the Outreach Program. I know it's Saturday night, so if you've got plans…"

"No, no, it's okay. Whatcha got?"

"There's this one little girl who's on suicide watch. She's past her twentieth week and tried to get an abortion but her family pressured her out of it. They're Christians and want her to have the baby but the guy who made her pregnant doesn't want to deal with the child support, and he's been threatening her. The Pastor was hoping we could talk to her."

"Sure, I'll go out. What time you want to meet at the church?"

"Would five be okay?"

"Fine, I'll see you then."

"Oh, Bree, I also had a family member who wanted to talk to you. I told him a little bit about you and he wanted to ask you a question. I can give you his number."

"All right," Bree jotted down the number. "I'm here at the office for most of the afternoon, I'll give him a call. See you at five."

Once again she considered the church obligation with mixed emotions. Her heart and soul assured her that it was her highest priority. Yet her mind was distracted by her budding relationship with Hoyt, her concern for his safety, and the crisis facing her Company. To top it off, Ryan's problem had now become part of a greater extortion scheme. Maybe Rita was going to be part of the answer for her. Sabrina needed moral support more than anything, and she actually did not have any close friends. Rita appeared as a kindred spirit who just might provide her with a shoulder to lean on in the weeks ahead.

"Hello?"

"Hi, this is Sabrina Brooks, I'm a friend of Rita Hunt. She gave me your number, she said you wanted to talk to me."

"Yes ma'am," the man's Kentuckian drawl was enthusiastic. "I'm James Hunt, I'm a distant cousin of Rita's. A friend of mine, Wayne Gladden, opened up a landscaping company down here in Bowling Green after we graduated high school, and we've done pretty well out here. We've done some work for a few ball clubs across Kentucky and we're kinda looking to expand a tad. Now, I understand you own a chemical company."

"Yes, sir, I do," she swiveled her chair and gazed out the window, kicking off her sneakers as she wore her hangout clothes like everyone else on weekends.

"I'm sure you're familiar with the problems they had up on the Jersey Shore recently, with that Hurricane Sandy and the flooding. Now, me and my partner Wayne have been contacting a few of the companies out there about a possible venture, and we have stirred up some interest. It's really in the iffy stage right now, but I think if we all join hands we can make something happen that can make us all some money and revitalize the Jersey Shore community."

"What'd you have in mind?"

"We were proposing a landscaped chain across the high-risk area. It would not only transform the aesthetics along the shoreline but provide a buffer should flooding or a water hazard occur again in the near future. The only setback is the continuing erosion that has deteriorated the natural soil along the coastline. We're thinking that a specially composed fertilizer used in conjunction with chemically treated soil might be able to accelerate plant growth and stabilize the environment."

"So you want me to develop fertilizer?"

"Miss Brooks, if we can put together a solid proposal, I'm thinking your end will be about five million dollars."

"Uh, yeah," she said nonchalantly, frantically scrambling through her desk drawer for a pen and paper. "I'd like to get together with my partner and my research team and look at that. Do you think you can put together a proposal with some figures so we can see if it's doable on our end?"

"Most certainly, Miss Brooks. Let me give you my e-mail address and I'll send you all the details."

"Sounds great," she scribbled it down. "I'll send you a ping, and you'll have mine."

"You know, I just wanted to say that Rita told me about the challenges you were facing as a female CEO. Anyone who could go out and do what you did for little Emma has more sand than ninety percent of the men I know. I'd trust you with a multimillion dollar project anytime."

"Did she tell you about the problem we had with that man and the thing on the news?"

"What man?" he scoffed before hanging up. "You call that a man?"

Sabrina was beside herself with exaltation and wanted to dance with joy. She wanted to run in and tell Jon but knew the best thing to do was look everything over and do the groundwork first. She wanted to firm up everything and make sure all the connections were solid. She would then call everyone in for a board meeting, just like her father would have done.

She would wait until then to tell Hoyt, and they would do something nice to celebrate.

She also realized that she had to keep from pressing too hard with Hoyt. She did not want to appear too pushy or make it looking like she needed a shoulder to cry on. She knew she may have been presumptuous in asking him to church, but it was something that had to be addressed. If he could not accept her as a churchgoer, then it would not work regardless of how much she liked him. At least they got past that, and all she could hope was that God would keep him out of harm's way this weekend.

"Sabrina?" Ryan reappeared in her doorway. "Gee, you're in a good mood."

"Oh, well, it's Saturday," she beamed. "Whatcha got?"

"I got in touch with my friend and told him what was happening. He says he'll talk to you," Ryan came over and put an envelope on her desk. "You know, I'm starting to suspect that they're planning to launder my own money through my own connection. Suppose they're getting everything in place to make me come up with a large sum, then run it through the Fund to make it look like I was moving my own money? If they stepped away, they'd make it look like I was misappropriating my own money."

"You know, that's a clever idea, but I think they're planning something just a little bit bigger," she assured him. "I'll give your friend a call."

Bree phoned Ryan's friend and agreed to meet him at Starbucks near NYU in an hour. She stopped in to Jon's office before preparing to leave.

"Don't forget, you've got that meeting with Tom Durham on Monday," he reminded her. "I'm still willing to go in your place, or tag along with you if you like." He still wore semi-casual clothes despite the fact everyone else was wearing jeans and sneakers. Jon's idea of casual was his corduroy blazer and loafers.

"You're making it sound like we're dead in the water either way, so what difference does it make?" she leaned against the doorframe.

"Well, it's just that he's an old-school construction guy, he's got that hardcore macho mentality," Jon steepled his fingers. "His idea of a power lunch is going down to a bar along the docks for beers and a game of pool. He's held a few important interviews at the shooting range, and he invites lots of his business associates to the gym with him. He liked your Dad because of the kind of man your father was, the way he carried himself. I don't think it's going to have a thing to do with you as a person, or wanting to continue doing business with BCC. He's just not going to be comfortable talking business with a woman. Your Dad didn't dare send Ryan or Rick to meet him, you could imagine what that would have been like."

"Tell you what," Sabrina came over to Jon's desk. "I don't want you brooding over this and having it spoil your weekend. Can you get him on the phone?"

Jon shrugged, then punched in a number and handed the phone to her.

"Tom Durham."

"Hi, Tom, it's Sabrina Brooks at BCC, how're you doing?"

"Just fine, young lady. I suppose we're still set for Monday?"

"Sure are. I was kinda wondering if you'd like to meet me over at the McBurney YMCA on 14th Street."

"Why, uh, sure."

"Do you have a pen? I can give you directions."

"No, I know where that is. I've been to the Judo Club there a couple of times."

"Great. See you then."

"Sabrina?" Jon exhaled after she hung up.

"Yeah?"

"Have a good weekend," he said dismissively, waving her off.

"See you Monday," she said merrily, prancing out the door.

Nat Osprey was a tall, bespectacled man who affably greeted Sabrina when she spotted him in his gray sports coat at Starbucks. They retired to a rear table where he explained his situation to her.

"Ryan and I called it quits a couple of years ago," Nat explained. "He wasn't able to make a commitment because he was married. It was before he started seeing Rick. We were seeing each other for about six months until we agreed the relationship wasn't going anywhere. We were both married, and we had too much to lose by trying to sneak around after work. We're still good friends, though, and when he explained to me what was happening, I told him I would try to help."

"You're going to be our best chance at finding these people," Sabrina assured him. "What I'm expecting is for them to try the connection after Ryan gives them the number and the access codes. They'd be fools to wait until the last minute. They'll probably try it once from an untraceable number, probably from a disposable cell phone. They'll try again from their secure line the day they're planning the transfer. They expect the transfer to take place in a matter of minutes, but hopefully it'll never happen. Here's my cell number. When you get the trace, just text your name in with the number. No one'll ever know you'd given it to me."

"Okay," he seemed slightly nervous. "If anyone ever finds out about this, my career is over. I've got a wife and four

kids as well as elderly parents to take care of."

"Have you and your wife made up?" she could not help herself. "Is everything okay at home now?"

"Everything's always been good with me and my wife," he replied quizzically. "We married as a matter of convenience. We both come from good families, we both have degrees, and our kids have a great future ahead of them. She doesn't meet all my sexual needs, and I think she's come to terms with that. She never had much of a desire in the first place, she's more of a breeder than a lover. I guess it's hard for a straight person to understand."

"I guess not," Sabrina agreed.

"Gotta go, dinner's at six," he looked at his watch. "Got some other stops to make. I'll put an SOS in front of my number if I come across anything."

"Cool beans," she smiled.

It was about six hours later when Nat Osprey, working from his home that evening, sent her an SOS with his number on it. She called him immediately and he gave her a phone number that would set off a cataclysmic chain of events in NYC.

She went to her knees in prayer and asked the Lord for guidance. When she asked for an alternative and none appeared to her, she could think of but one solution.

The Nightcrawler would return to action.

Chapter Five

It was determined that the foiled attack had been designed to take advantage of a shift in trade winds that would have carried the anthrax powder across the shore into the Wall Street area. Analysts estimated that as much as ninety five percent of the germs would have dissipated along the harbor, but the highly potent virus strain would have contaminated the Statue itself. Any anthrax that would have survived the journey across the river would have been highly toxic and could have easily started a minor outbreak.

The State prosecution found itself immediately on the defensive as the terrorists' ACLU lawyers charged that their gay rights had been violated in uncovering the plot. The women, Lana Harper and Mindy Harris, had accessed a secured phone line to the Gotham AIDS Fund before the attack. The ACLU charged that their privacy had been violated, and the Nightcrawler had somehow traced the call in order to discover their identities. Moreover, the vigilante was able to hack the women's personal computer to steal information that led to the attack against them at the Statue of Liberty.

Both Harper and Harris maintained that they had been scammed by a group calling itself the Octagon that met them at the Statue with a briefcase full of travelogues that would enable them to sell tourist packages to visitors. Somehow the terrorists had switched the suitcase with them, and the women were attacked by the Nightcrawler in the Statue's torch where they were framed for the crime.

Officer Hoyt Wexford, who was on duty at the scene of the crime, had been given a taped confession by the Nightcrawler shortly after the incident ended. The ACLU, after a medical examination, obtained evidence that an experimental drug called DAT-KO had been used on the women to disable them and extract their confessions. It was determined that the gas had decreased their mental responsiveness with its shock effect on their dopaminergic systems. It acted as a sophisticated truth serum that left them defenseless against the Nightcrawler's interrogation.

Harper and Harris were being held without bail at the Attica Correctional Facility awaiting trial for terrorism under the New York Anti-Terror Laws. The NYPD, though having an all-points alert out on the Nightcrawler, were exultant over the intel provided on the tape given Wexford by the vigilante. They had made copies of it as well as electronic transcripts, and though the ACLU had the tape handed over to the court, the info was distributed throughout the Department's databases. A SWAT team had descended on the warehouse hideout of the Octagon shortly after the women gave up the location, but it had been deserted hours before their arrival.

Sabrina Brooks had been so shaken by the incident that she nearly called off from work the next day. She had suffered multiple contusions during the series of events that occurred on Sunday, and had barely made it back to the family manor in one piece. She felt so bad that she switched off her cell phone and her land line, and laid on her couch in the dark until the pounding on the front door forced her to respond late Sunday evening.

"Hello, Hoyt," she managed as she opened the door. She was so exhausted and sore that she had not even smoothed her hair out before answering.

"Bree," he was surprised by her disheveled appearance. He was just as wearied himself, having experienced one of the longest days in his career though casually dressed in his undercover attire. "I've been calling you for hours. I thought something was wrong, you've never left your cell phone off before. I'm sorry for coming over like this, but I got worried about you."

"No, I'm fine, just a little bit under the weather," she assured him. "Come on in."

He was greatly concerned as she walked with a heavy limp to the wall switch to the enormous chandelier illuminating the Spanish-style living room. He sat in an armchair across from her as she lowered herself painfully onto the couch.

"Geez, were you in an accident? What happened?"

"Well, yeah, kind of," she tried to explain. "There was a bird stuck up on the roof, it looked like he hurt his wing. Stupid me, I went and got a ladder and climbed up to get him. When I went to pick him up he started flapping his wings and managed to fly off. I got startled and rolled right off the roof. I guess all that rolling around on the mat came in handy, but I kinda sprained my leg."

"You got to be more careful, doll. I guess you haven't watched any TV today, huh?"

"No, I've been feeling pretty bad," she managed a smile.

"That Nightcrawler guy turned up again at the Statue of Liberty," he studied her face intently. "You wouldn't believe how it went down. It just so happened I had been assigned there to keep an eye on the crowd in case there was any activity."

"Oh my gosh," Sabrina's eyes widened. "Are you okay? Was there a problem?"

"Well, yeah," he rubbed his chin. "Matter of fact, a couple of women showed up at the Statue with a satchel filled with a concentrated anthrax powder. They went up to the torch and were going to dump the powder over the side. They were expecting the wind to blow it into the Wall Street area. The Department thinks it was more of a calculated threat than anything since there's no way in hell the powder could've carried that far. Anyway, the Nightcrawler found out about it somehow and stopped them from dumping the powder. He also got a taped statement from them which he personally handed to me before going back up into the torch."

"So did everything go okay? Did you get in trouble for not arresting him?"

"Actually I pulled my weapon and ordered him to stop but he kept on running up the steps. My only option was to shoot him in the back. I followed him up just as a helicopter with a rope ladder had come for the terrorists. He jumped on the ladder, and when they saw what happened they tried to cut him loose. I cuffed the terrorists and called for backup, and while I did, the Nightcrawler went into the river. By the time the patrol boats arrived, he disappeared. The Coast Guard is still searching for a body, but I'm betting he got away."

"My gosh, you must be up for some kind of reward for arresting those terrorists," she gushed happily. "Now you're my hero, that's for sure."

"The big problem right now is the Nightcrawler, believe it or not. He used some kind of nerve gas on the terrorists to get their statement. Plus he used an illegal trace to tap into their computer system to find out about the attack. Right now they're looking for him as if he was one of the terrorists."

"Isn't that something," she shook her head. "Well, you'll probably never hear from him again. He'd be crazy to come back out again after something like that."

"You know, what was really crazy was when he came down that stairwell. The security people were keeping the tourists back after I flashed my badge when the stuff hit the fan. I got this weird feeling of déjà vu, almost like I knew this guy. You know like when you're in a crowd and one of your friends or family are there, and even though you can't see them you know they're there? Well, it was kinda like that."

"Wow, I'll bet that sure was something," she nodded.

"Bree?"

"Yeah?"

"You wouldn't know who that Nightcrawler is, if it's one of the guys?"

"Why, no! Why would you think that?"

"Well, the thing about the chemical weapons. There's no way you would let anyone have anything like that, even if they were using it for good."

"I kinda hate to bust your bubble there, fellow," she chuckled, "but one of the girls from church had a relative call me the other day, and we're discussing a contract to develop a fertilizer. I'm afraid we're not quite at the chemical weapon level just yet."

"I'm sorry," he pinched the bridge of his nose, falling back in his chair. "My mind's turning to mush, I don't know what I'm thinking. They took me downtown and grilled me like I was one of the gang. I had to repeat the story to my sergeant, then the lieutenant, and finally to Captain Willard. I filled out so many forms I think I got carpal tunnel. They had the FBI and Homeland Security over at Police Plaza trying to make our guys look like the Keystone Kops. I went through so many changes today it was unreal. Not to mention finding this place."

"That's okay. Let me make you something to eat."

"No, I gotta go," he pushed himself to his feet. "I'm beat to heck. I'm gonna have trouble keeping my eyes open. Good thing there's hardly any traffic."

"How about some coffee?"

"Next time. How about Wednesday? I can come by and meet you after work, I'll buy you dinner."

"Sounds great," her eyes twinkled as she hobbled to the door alongside him.

"You take care of yourself, okay," he smiled, her face angelic in the moonlight.

"You too."

He took her by the shoulders gently and kissed her cheek. She closed her eyes and felt her heart skip a beat as he waved and trotted down the brick pathway across the lawn to his Lexus.

It would be so much easier to go to sleep now, with cotton candy clouds floating around her head and Hoyt Wexford as her guardian angel.

When she came to work the next day, she found that Ryan Hoffman had called off and that Jon Aeppli had been trying to call her at home. She had called the answering service to get her messages, and decided to weed through the clot of messages on her voicemail at the office. Her left leg was black and blue and she could barely move her left arm, but she rubbed herself down with Ben-Gay before going in to face the music.

She wore a pants suit for a change, normally favoring her Neiman Marcus skirt suits which showed off her legs and were much cooler throughout the day. Today her left leg looked like purple haze, and it would probably be a couple of days before she tried a dress suit with opaque nylons. It was exceedingly difficult to walk without a limp, and she decided on wearing flat heels which was another anomaly for her.

"Morning, Jon."

"Have a seat. Close the door," his gold-rimmed glasses were balanced on the end of his sloped nose as he looked down at his paperwork.

"Hey, I thought I was the boss around here," she managed a chuckle.

"You're gonna be running this place all by yourself pretty soon," he stared up at her.

"What?" she took a shot at playing dumb.

"I thought we agreed there would be no more Nightcrawler."

"Jon, I didn't have a choice. I got some reliable information that terrorists were planning an attack on the Wall Street area. If I would've called it in, it would've gone viral and the terrorists would've saved the anthrax weapon for a rainy day. I took a chance and managed to take out the terrorists. The Government knows about the Octagon now. Homeland Security will find these guys without the Nightcrawler. I'm done now for good."

"So am I. Sabrina, I was at the hospital when you were born. Your father let me hold you when they brought you home, and I'll never forget that look in his eye. He had that look when you graduated grade school and high school, and when you enrolled at NYU. You and your Mom were the most important

42

things in his life, more important than this Company. I'm not gonna stay here and keep this place open after you're gone. There'd be no sense in it."

"I'm begging you, you can't leave. I'd be suicidal," her eyes grew moist.

"And you're not now?" he tossed his glasses onto the desk. "The police estimated that the Nightcrawler plummeted three hundred and fifty feet into the East River after being cut loose from the terrorists' helicopter. How's your leg feeling?"

"Well, I made it to work."

"I suppose you told that undercover officer you've been seeing. I heard he was the one you gave that taped confession to."

"No, you're the only one who knows. He'd probably stop seeing me if he knew."

"He'd probably force you to seek psychiatric treatment. Speaking of which, have you heard anything about those women you gassed?"

"Who, those killers?" she flared.

"Sabrina, you cannot use DATKO on the field, not in that untested state. It's extremely dangerous. You might cause someone permanent brain damage."

"Jon, we're talking about people who were about to unleash a dirty bomb near the Wall Street area. Don't you think there's an opportunity cost to be considered?"

"There's just too much on the table here," he exhaled. "I can't be a part of this."

"So you're gonna walk away and leave me hanging with Tom Durham's project? And what about the e-mail I sent you about James Hunt's project?"

"What about it?" he challenged her. "You're supposed to meet Tom Durham at the YMCA at noon."

"Yeah. So?"

"You know how much your father hated that answer with that tone of voice? I'm starting to see why."

"Okay, so if I go, and I get the contract, will you stay and help?"

"I'll say this. I've buried your mother and I buried your father. I am not going to bury you, and I'd see you in prison before I watch you get yourself killed. You need to understand that."

"So you won't snitch on me this time?"

"Go on," he waved his hand as if dismissing an unruly student, waving his hand. "Get out of here. Tell Tom Durham I said hello."

"I sure will," she bit her lip as she got up on her bad leg.

"And another thing."

"Yeah?"

"I hope he knocks you on your ass."

Sabrina drove out to the YMCA at noon and met with Tom Durham. He was a powerfully-built man at 5'9", 210 pounds, his thick black hair and mustache graying along the sides. He was taken aback when she suggested they work out together, and even more so when she mentioned putting on the gloves.

"They ran me off from the YMCA in Chinatown, so I figured I'd give this place a try, especially since they have the judo team," she said amiably. "I was hoping we could just move around, I wouldn't want you to take my head off."

"Okay," he grunted reluctantly. "Now, do you have one of those catcher's chest guards, or one of them armored bras? You're kinda big on top, you know."

"Ye—ah," she raised an eyebrow. "You got your noseguard, you know, your cup? You might be kinda big downstairs, I can't tell."

They went in and signed up, then changed clothes and met in the open floor area by the mats. A couple of attendants looked over and decided that the older man had brought his daughter in to teach her how to defend herself. They were left to themselves, though more than one visitor was surprised at the intensity of the session. After about a half hour, both boxers noticed the time and mutually agreed to hit the showers.

Sabrina met Durham out front, and Tom had a big grin on his face. He patted her on the back and shook her hand.

"Well, you sure are Vern Brooks' daughter, that's for damn sure."

"You've got a great left jab right hook combo," she said admiringly. "I sure am glad you were taking it easy on me."

"Let me tell you something, sweetheart. When I started blowing up, I was throwing it in hard to keep you off me. You're a helluva boxer. Don't get any crazy ideas about making money at it, though. You don't wanna mess up that face of yours. You look like a movie star."

"Gee, thanks," she blushed.

"Okay, so look," he mused. "We're looking at some contracting work along the Brooklyn Bridge. They're forever getting potholes and want a crew to bring something to the table to prove it's gonna stay fixed for a reasonable amount of time. They're coming in at $150 million, and if I go with you and bid $140, I can get you fourteen mil on your end. Don't forget, though, this stuff we lay down there needs to last."

"Sure," she tried to maintain her composure. "Uh, if you can just e-mail everything over to me, I'll get together with Jon and the guys, and we'll send a proposal over as soon as possible."

"Sounds good. Keep that right up, watch that kisser."

"Sure will."

She had met with Rita Hunt that Saturday evening after her meeting with Nat Osprey. They went together to visit Lindsay White at the Bowery Mission Women's Shelter at Heartsease Home. Lindsay was in her fifth month of pregnancy and hiding out from her boyfriend, who was demanding that she abort to spare him eighteen years of child support. She swore that she would never ask him for a dime, but he assured her that they would come after him regardless of her wishes once they determined he was the father. She went into hiding when he told her that either she would abort or he would do it for her.

Lindsay was a pretty girl with Dutch girl features, flaxen blonde hair with pinkish skin and a cherubic countenance. She had big blue Bette Davis crying eyes, and Sabrina's heart immediately went out to her. The women were checked in at the front desk and a matron escorted Lindsay out to the lobby to meet them.

"I don't want to kill my baby," Lindsay sobbed as she told her tale to Sabrina. Rita already knew what was going on, and held her hand in consolation. "I understand what he's telling me, that anything can happen in eighteen years, but isn't a human life more important? Is this child never going to see the sun shine, never hear a bird sing, or never have a birthday or a Christmas just because someone can't afford it?"

"No, don't you worry about it," Sabrina insisted. "I have a business that isn't doing too badly right now. You go ahead and have that baby, and we'll make sure it gets adopted into a good Christian home that is praying to be blessed with a newborn."

"See, that's the downside," Rita told her. "It costs about ten thousand dollars to go through the adoption process, with all the paperwork involved. Most Christian families simply don't have that kind of money before taking on the expense of raising a child."

"Well, we'll see about that," Sabrina mulled it over. "If someone were to donate the money to a Church that would give the money over for humanitarian purposes, then I would think someone's got some pretty good tax write-offs coming, don't you?"

"Gee, that's an idea," Rita's eyes lit up.

"The only jam I see might be the Church donating it for the cause, but if the IRS decided to have a go at them, they would have to prove that rescuing a child from an orphanage is not a humanitarian act. And if they went after Pastor Mitchell, they'd have to get through BCC's lawyers. That'd be a pay-per-view matchup, in my book."

"Well, I'd run it by the Pastor and see what he says," Rita decided. "I'm pretty sure Lindsay wouldn't have a problem with it."

"Oh, thank you, thank you!" Lindsay wept with gladness, throwing her arms around Sabrina.

It felt a lot better than singlehandedly beating down two steroid-fueled lesbians at the Statue of Liberty.

Rita and Sabrina went to meet with the Pastor Monday night, and he seemed eager to go provided that all the legal groundwork was tended to beforehand. Sabrina promised that she would meet with her lawyers to ensure that everything would be taken care of. She next called her CPA and asked him to explore the tax shelters available for companies donating to humanitarian causes in NYC. After that, she drove back to the BCC campus to meet with Jon Aeppli.

"Okay, so you're thinking the addition of a heat-resistant hot-melt pressure sensitive adhesive is gonna make this work if we can combine it with the asphalt sealant compound," Jon looked at the report and worksheets Sabrina had come up with. "So you're thinking of using the styrene sec-butyllithium as the prepolymerized catalyst?"

"Well," she said tentatively, "if we remove the cyclohexane to give it the ABA type block copolymer, plus with the A dosage and B mixing, I think it might be what Tom's looking for."

"I'll take this home and kick it around, tweak it up and run it by Rick and Ryan," Jon exhaled. "Fifteen million, what's he got in mind, paving up through Memorial Park to Borough Hall?"

"I think he's looking at possible trial-and-error, possible setbacks and profit margins," she shrugged. "I don't see why we can't come up with one hundred and sixteen thousand gallons of this stuff for much more than eight million dollars. That should be enough to coat the Bridge and have enough left over for a couple of miles on the inroads."

"I think you missed your calling."

"I agree. I should've been a superhero."

"I didn't mean that," Jon frowned at her as his cell phone went off. "You should've went into construction, it's obviously better money—hello, this is Jon."

Sabrina watched as he walked over to his desk, picked up his remote control, and switched on the rarely-used wide-screen plasma TV dominating the far wall of his office space.

"Barbara called, she says we ought to see this."

Jon tuned in to CNN at the behest of his wife and saw a replay of a prerecorded tape that had been broadcast via satellite through Cuba from an undisclosed location. The figure of a powerfully-built blond man in a tank-top sat behind a desk before a shadowy backdrop, his face electronically distorted.

"The people of New York City must realize that they are in a war that they cannot win," the man declared. "Their battle is being fought by cowardly incompetents who do not have the skill or the will to defeat a superior opponent who will never give up before victory is achieved. This is not Boston, where an entire city and state consolidated its resources with that of its citizens to defeat two simple-minded adolescents. Think of the terrible tragedy you endured just a little over a decade ago on 9/11. Stopping us at the Statue of Liberty was merely a minor setback. This time, we are demanding ten million dollars as payment in dissuading us from turning your oceanfront into blood. If our demands are not met within forty-eight hours, we will make good on our promise."

"Oh my goodness," Sabrina's eyes widened. "That must be the Reaper."

The CNN journalist announced that Al-Qaeda denied having any connections to the Octagon and would never solicit or extort money for a military action undertaken in the name of Allah. He also received word that the Cuban government confirmed they had merely acted as a broadcast platform for the Octagon and denied any association with the terrorist group.

"If they developed an anthrax weapon they literally scattered to the four winds to demonstrate their capability, we can only imagine what they're planning next," Jon was somber as he switched off the TV.

"They've got to be in the chemical business, or know somebody who does," Sabrina mused.

"They could be getting the weapons from overseas," Jon pointed out. "It could be Syria, North Korea, Iran, or even Russia."

"Why would they let them take that kind of chance in dumping the product? Suppose Homeland Security was able to trace some of the compounding

agents? If there was an identifiable enzyme characteristic of a foreign manu-
facturer—"

"The news reports haven't indicated whether or not Homeland Security was
able to get any information from whatever must have been left in that briefcase," Jon surmised. "Chances are they sent it to a police lab. We know they
wouldn't do the same quality analysis as a mainstream company."

"I'll bet I know someone who could get me a sample."

"You're not afraid of risking your relationship? You might even run the risk
of him being obligated to turn you in."

"He can't arrest what he can't catch. I was thinking Nightcrawler."

"Did you not promise me—!"

"I didn't say I was jumping off the Statue of Liberty, I'm only wearing a
disguise to go visit Hoyt!"

"There's no use in trying," he waved her off as he headed out the door. "I'll
look over your paperwork on the Durham deal and have it ready by tomorrow
morning."

Jon's statement hit Sabrina like a punch in the tummy. She realized she would
be taking a major risk in losing the man she was falling in love with. Only
the lives of

innocent civilians might be at risk if she did not do so.

She saw no alternative but to turn to Pastor Mitchell and see if God would
help her find a way.

Chapter Six

One week after the failed attempt to saturate the air above the Wall Street area with anthrax, Tommie Pressley and Kyle De Lorean were arrested on Manhattan Beach for violations of the Anti-Terror Act. Impersonating lifeguards on the crowded beach, they were apprehended before being able to detonate 500-pound shrapnel bombs hidden beneath their tower posts. The Coast Guard intercepted an oil tanker a mile from the beach bearing Syrian insignia and markings that was filled with Agent BZ in a liquid compound.

The City, the nation and the world were horrified at the deviousness of the plot. The casualty rate would have dwarfed that of the Boston Massacre as thousands of bathers had packed the beach to enjoy the perfect spring weather. The explosions were designed to drive the survivors into the water, where they would have waded directly into the waves of Agent BZ being washed upon the shore. The swarms of emergency rescue teams would have clogged the boardwalk, causing more people to be pushed back towards the water to be ravaged by the toxic chemicals. It would have a catastrophe of epic proportions had the terrorists not been thwarted in time.

Sabrina Brooks had visited Pastor Matt Mitchell again after meeting with him and Rita Hunt earlier that week. The Pastor was greatly interested in her proposal to provide financial backing for Christian couples interested in adopting. He agreed to wait for further word from her lawyer and her accountant before making any moves on his end. He expected Sabrina to be coming by the Church with the latest developments, but was astounded to hear of her exploits as the Nightcrawler instead. Just as she told Jon Aeppli, she had been too traumatized by the City Administration's backlash against the Nightcrawler and did not plan on going out again.

Only when she had hacked into the Octagon's computer and downloaded their database, she went to considerable expense to have the encrypted files translated. She hired five of the top computer geniuses in the country to analyze separate files, and the first one who proved successful was awarded the job of cracking the entire database. She paid fifty thousand dollars out of her own savings for the service, though seriously compromising her long-term financial security in having cashed in some of her 401k accounts. Yet now she could see what the Octagon had planned for their next attack, and was able to formulate a plan to cause their downfall.

Pressley and De Lorean suspected that their computer system had been hacked, and fiercely presented their case before the Octagon at their meeting before the attack on Manhattan Beach. The absence of Harper and Harris at the team's nonagonal table in their Catskills Mountain stronghold was as a rebuke and a disgrace to the team. Pressley and De Lorean's angry denouement of the debacle only served to increase tensions at the table.

"There's no way the mission wasn't compromised!" Pressley railed as the other members listened moodily. "How could this guy have known to ambush the girls just before the wind picked up enough for them to dump the powder? We had the whole operation timed for them to be in and out in thirty minutes. They got inside, made it to the top, cleared everyone out of the torch area, and were ready to unload just when this guy shows up. I'm thinking that Ryan Hoffman reached out to him at some point, that's the only possibility. And if that's the case, then how can we not overlook the possibility that our inside contact hasn't been compromised?"

"I can guarantee that our operative is beyond reproach," the person known as Scorpion spoke up. Both the Scorpion and the Tarantula were the Reaper's top lieutenants, and wore masks and distortion mics to the summit meetings. Like the others, they were the head of their own gangs, but remained part of the Octagon as it continued earning millions of dollars through its underworld ventures. "The contact assured us that Hoffman made no contact with the police. The contact had Hoffman under surveillance the entire time and even had his home phone tapped. Whoever found out about Harris and Harper must have infiltrated their networks somehow. They are the only ones who can provide the answers we seek."

"Harris and Harper are both in solitary confinement in Attica, so we might as well just forget about any input from them for a long time to come," Vincent

Gargano spoke up. He and his partner, Walt Griffin, were explosives experts with the US Army in Iraq who were discharged long before the American military stood up for gay rights. They eagerly accepted the Reaper's offer when they returned home, and became millionaires within a year of their enrollment with the Octagon. They were both bisexuals, and easily negotiated their way between both worlds as the Octagon's interests dictated.

"I don't like the fact there's a secret contact," Griffin insisted. "It's been said that we are all equals here, though we have accepted the leadership of the Reaper and his delegates. If that's the case, then we should know who the insider is. Suppose one of the rest of us knows something about him or her that you three don't? And suppose one of us is compromised and we decide to hold back information on the source until it's too late? This is setting a dangerous precedent and it may cause us all to reconsider our positions here. We've got enough to worry about the Government sending Harris and Harper to Guantanamo to force information out of them."

"Do you question our judgment of character?" the Scorpion demanded.

"What, is that supposed to scare me?" Gargano lisped.

"Gentlemen," the Reaper raised his voice. "We have not come here to recriminate or second-guess ourselves. This is the first time one of our operations has failed, and the first time any of our people have been apprehended. Divulging the identity of our inside source would serve no purpose whatsoever. If this person were to be compromised, our WMD capability would be seriously impaired. Everyone was aware of the risks involved when we undertook his mission. There is no need to increase the risk by possibly exposing our inside source."

"Okay, keep your little rat hidden wherever it is," Pressley waved a hand. "What do you intend to do about the leak? That Nightcrawler found out about our Manhattan hideout the same way he found out about the operation. Ryan Hoffman is the only one who was able to put two and two together. I say we bring him in and make him give up the Nightcrawler."

"Can't you see it works both ways?" the Reaper insisted. "If the Nightcrawler finds out we've gotten onto Hoffman, he may disappear completely. Right now, the two of them may be the only ones who think they have a chance of stopping us. We know the Nightcrawler is not working with the authorities, they've got a manhunt going for him. If this vigilante has any more information about us, we have to lure him in and finish him off before we reach the advanced stages of our mission."

"Hoffman is nothing but a stepping stone along our road to destiny!" the Tarantula hissed. "We have already burned the bridge that the Nightcrawler accessed, our tracks have been covered. We have no way of knowing of the relationship between Hoffman and the Nightcrawler. The Reaper is right, if we move against Hoffman, we don't know what the Nightcrawler has on us. If he turns it over to the Government, we don't know if it will be enough to end our mission. I say we bide our time and let this fool make his next move."

"How can we know if he hasn't notified the Government already!" De Lorean exclaimed.

"Because our stockpile of Agent BZ hasn't been captured, dear friends!" the Reaper retorted. "The video is set to be delivered to City Hall tonight. The entire world will know of our demands. If they do not send the ten million to our Cuban connection, the people of Brooklyn will suffer a devastation unseen since Sodom and Gomorrah!"

"Too bad they won't have as much fun before it happens," Gargano said slyly, evoking a hearty round of laughter from his partners.

Sabrina Brooks knew she was in a race against time, yet her personal life was in such a state of agitation that she dared not set it aside. Hoyt Wexford called to cancel their dinner date for Wednesday, yet they agreed to meet for lunch near NYU just to spend whatever time they could together. They were both just started to realize how much they missed each other, and suspected this was turning into something more than a close friendship. The electricity that ran through the big embrace they exchanged when they met said it all.

"I don't know what this world's coming to, Bree," Hoyt picked at his plate desultorily. "You know, neither Al Qaeda nor the Chechens sent advance notice of a second attack. These maniacs obviously aren't afraid of getting caught. Even more obviously they think they're gonna get away with it."

"It'll be okay," she said encouragingly. "They stopped them last time without knowing it was coming. This time they'll be ready. They'll put the whole bunch of them away forever. You'll see, you're gonna miss out on all that overtime."

"They're just trying to figure out how that Nightcrawler knew," he looked at her oddly. "If only he'd come forward and tell them what he knows."

"You know, you got this look in your eye—"

"No," he raised his hand. "No, no, I'm sorry. I know you would've told me if you knew anything. You trained with us at John Jay, you know what all of us are facing out there against these guys. I know you'd never hold back if it could save lives. You're too wonderful a person for anyone to even think otherwise."

When they parted, they hugged and kissed each other's cheek, and she felt like a schoolgirl wondering what it would be like when he kissed her on the lips. He told her he would call her Saturday, but neither of them dreamed they would be involved in the chaos of Manhattan Beach.

She had reached out once again to Nat Osprey without Ryan Hoffman's knowledge. Ryan had gone through some major changes after the extortion threat by the Octagon. He had begun scheduling vacation time in one-day increments, whereas he had normally taken his full month off around Labor Day to go on a trip with his wife and kids. He also seemed nervous and distracted where he had always been cheerful and energetic. Sabrina had tried to talk to him but he continued to assure her that he just needed time to get back to normal.

Nat was just as uncertain in dealing with Sabrina, but he realized the predicament she had put herself in. If she revealed her secret identity, there was a strong possibility that BCC could be closed down for the manufacture of chemical weapons. Yet if she remained on the sidelines, her failure to act might result in an opening for the Octagon's next move. He was in a similar situation in that his refusal to cooperate could result in the death of innocent victims if the Octagon's attack proved successful.

"If we could just take a look at all the calls from the Middle East to the New York area, we might be able to narrow it down," Sabrina insisted as they met at Starbucks near NYU once again. "Look, this isn't going to be done in just a couple of calls. They can't be relying entirely on e-mail because of the Homeland Security monitoring. Plus this isn't going to be something in the planning stages. This is a done deal, and what they would be doing at this point is making last-minute confirmations. If we could just get a handle on one call, just one call—!"

"Sabrina, I'm on your side all the way," Nat cleared his throat. "It's that I'm just as scared as Ryan, and for all the same reasons. If they ever found out, I'd not only lose my job but I could be facing jail time for FCC violations. They'd hang me out to dry and my whole life would be destroyed. If they ever found out about me and Ryan, or any of the guys I've dated, my wife would divorce me and my kids would disown me. There's a difference between your family thinking you might be queer and the whole world finding out for sure. Not to mention the lives of all the other guys."

"All we need to know is what Middle East shipping firms have made any calls to private numbers here in the States," she pleaded. "When we confirm calls to family or friends, the list would be narrowed down by seventy-five percent. If we looked at calls that went from land lines to mobile numbers since last Sunday, we'd know that it was because they knew we traced their call back to their hideout, and they wouldn't let it happen again. If we could come up with a short list, all we'd have to do is find out who has ships scheduled to arrive in New York this weekend. Nat, you can help me figure this out, please!"

"This is going to be the last time, this is the end of the line for me," Nat wiped his brow. "I want you to swear to me you'll never reach out to me again after this. I know you're a church person, that's one of the reasons I agreed with Ryan to help you. Now you need to swear to me that this is the last time. No more, never again. Deal?"

"Deal," she exhaled tautly.

She was feeling more and more isolated as it seemed everyone was turning their backs on her. Jon Aeppli was finally becoming more understanding, but still insisted she had to give this up at the end of the day. She agreed with Jon that if Hoyt were to find out, it could mean his career if he did not arrest her. Pastor Mitchell believed she had to let it go as well. The only other person who knew her secret was Nat, and she swore that their connection would be ended after this. If she did not take the Octagon down once and for all, she would be all alone against them.

The only source of encouragement she was getting was from her Church family, and ironically she had not been to church in almost a month. She felt a sense of satisfaction in knowing that her tithe of ten percent of her salary had to be paying a lot of bills. Yet she wanted to get more involved, though she knew she was entering uncharted waters in helping set up the adoption service. If everything did not go as planned it would let a lot of people down, not to mention the trauma it would cause in the lives of girls like Lindsay White.

Rita Hunt called that Wednesday and she was as buoyant and optimistic as always. She told Sabrina that Lindsay's ex had agreed to allow her to have the baby provided the adoption was set in stone before the delivery. Everyone was both relieved and exhilarated save for Sabrina, who did not have anything confirmed by the lawyer or CPA yet. She had already given up fifty grand in hiring the hacker to decode the Octagon files, and now she was likely to eat thirty grand in legal fees if they weren't able to divert the expense into a tax shelter. She had some nice money coming in with Tom Durham and James Hunt, but she hadn't even seen the pens that would sign those contracts yet.

"Bree, honey, the other girls are feeling real good about the project," Rita assured her as they chatted on the phone that evening. "Almost every one of them were considering abortion, but after the Pastor and the other sisters counseled them, they started thinking twice about taking the lives of their own children. Now that they know there's an option of having them adopted so the fathers aren't bearing the burden, it's opened their eyes to a new reality."

"I'm so glad," Sabrina gushed, though hoping she had not bit off more than she could chew. "I think if we just keep them prayed up and remind them that we're gonna be there for them, everything'll work out just fine."

"Let's just remember that God is in control," Rita reminded her, as if sensing Sabrina's concerns. "If things don't work out, then it wasn't meant to be. We can't blame ourselves, we can only do our best, then let go and let God."

Thursday morning she decided to get Ryan back into the game, appointing him to take charge of the Jersey Shore project while Rick Alfonso was given charge of the Brooklyn Bridge overhaul. Though she realized that she and Jon would be doing most of the heavy lifting in the long run and making the crucial decisions, giving Ryan and Rick the responsibility and the credit would go a long way in building morale and team spirit. It also freed Jon up in case she needed his input as the deadline set by the Octagon drew near.

She had decided not to attempt to reach out to Hoyt as the Nightcrawler. It would compromise what she considered one of her most important relationships. She knew that she and Hoyt were bonding so that he would be able to see right through her uniform if she wore it before him once more. She would take advantage of this next encounter with the Octagon to take them down. If she did not succeed then she would get enough evidence to hand over to the police to finish the job.

"I think you're making a wise decision," Jon assured her. "You may have a good thing going with Hoyt. He's got his own career, he won't feel resentful of your success. Plus, as time goes by, I think you'll be getting a vicarious satisfaction from his achievements in law enforcement. We both know that your gift for chemistry might come in useful as a resource for him. The police often solve cases by referring to outside sources in analyzing clues and forensics evidence."

It was not long after Jon left for the evening when she got her last helping hand from Nat Osprey. He called her on her cell phone and seemed nervous in providing the information, apparently concerned by the possibility that either the police or the Octagon might have gotten wise to Sabrina.

"I nearly cut to the chase and almost cut my own throat in the process," Nat grew hoarse at the thought. "Homeland Security had already confiscated our records to trace all the calls to the terrorists' hideout. If I would've gone in behind them they would've caught me red-handed. I took a different approach and started looking at oil companies. They would be the least likely to compromise their favored trade status. I hit lightning in a bottle with the Chammoun Petroleum Company. They made dozens of calls to a Mexican company in El Paso that was also acting as a switch for a satellite hookup in Havana, Cuba."

"Omigosh," she remembered that the Octagon's Monday night video transmission had been sent from a switch in Cuba.

"I'm done here, Sabrina," Osprey said before hanging up. "I wish you the best of luck."

She next went into her father's contact database and the company's business records, searching for contracts and bids with companies in the South Texas area. She found a Laredo Oil and Gas Resources with offices in El Paso, and decided to take a chance.

"Hi, this is Sabrina Brooks, Vern's daughter," she began calling at eight AM on Friday morning, which was seven AM in Texas. She was transferred and placed on hold innumerable times, and finally got Rod Ramirez on his cell phone. "I'm trying to get some information about the Chammoun Petroleum Company out of Damascus, and I was wondering if you could help me."

"I'll do the best I can. Sabrina, I sure was sorry to hear about your Dad. He was a great man and it was always a pleasure doing business with him."

"He always spoke highly of you, and that's why I thought I might be able to come to you. I was even thinking that if this deal with Chammoun Petroleum didn't work out, maybe you and I could do business."

"I'm all ears."

"Well, we were doing work with polymers in another project with a New York construction company. Word of mouth got back to Chammoun, and they approached us with an offer to develop a polymer-based dispersant in the event that the rebels in Syria begin sabotaging their off-shore facilities. The numbers looked good, but when we started checking their references things got murky.

I'm thinking they might be a dummy corporation for some operation that might leave us high and dry on the back end of the deal. What I'm trying to find out is if they have any of their freighters or tankers taking a detour to New York from El Paso on the way back to the Middle East. If they're rerouting deliveries to circumvent the embargo, I don't want anything to do with them."

"Very interesting," Ramirez mused. "I would be very interested in investing in chemical dispersant research. I wouldn't want to profit from the misfortune of a competitor, but illegal activity in our industry works to the detriment of one and all. Now, obviously if the Chammouns are operating here in El Paso, they must have some connections in Juarez. And, of course, so do I. I can have some people do some deep digging for you, but of course there will be a service fee involved. We can exchange e-mails and I will send you the details."

"I'm sure you'll give me a fair price. All I ask is that you can have your people check this out at their earliest convenience. They're giving us a take-it-or-leave-it deadline, and I would've dropped it flat if I wasn't trying to keep the company moving ahead, you know, with my father's passing."

"I understand, my dear. Let me see what I can put together, and we will find out whether or not these Chammouns would honor their end of the deal with BCC."

By Thursday afternoon, Ramirez paid $5,000 in advance on Sabrina's behalf to a Mexican company who had arranged to purchase a shipment of oil on a Panamax tanker carrying 500,000 barrels from Bantas, Syria that would be sold to American companies as Mexican oil. As she suspected, the tanker was taking a circular rout past Florida towards New York en route to the UK. Although it was cutting heavily into the inheritance left by her mother, she gladly paid Ramirez for the information that would help her develop a game plan.

Sabrina next contacted a local yacht and boat charter service, renting a boat for sightseeing purposes for a one-person trip. The boat operator was some-what suspicious when the female passenger arrived in Muslim attire with a veiled face. He was even more anxious when the woman produced a modified GPS and asked that the operator sail according to its coordinates. A hundred-dollar tip assuaged him temporarily until they began nearing an oil tanker that was veering suspiciously close to Manhattan Beach at Coney Island.

She explained that she was doing a news expose and needed to get close enough to photograph the ship's markings. When he got her within ten yards, he was astonished to see that her tripod case actually contained a modified harpoon. She fired the weapon at the side of the ship and used the rappelling gear beneath her robes to pull her onto the tanker after she dived off the ship.

The operator, aghast at the thought of being involved in a terror attack, immediately notified the police and the Coast Guard. By the time they arrived, the Nightcrawler had subdued the twelve-man crew and used her DATKO nerve gas to learn of Pressley and De Lorean's role in the plot. She called 911 and told them she spotted two bogus lifeguards unloading suspicious equipment at the stations near Manhattan Beach Park. The NYPD was already on the scene, and arrested the Octagon terrorists before they were able to activate the shrapnel bombs.

She finally returned home that evening and found her answering machine and cell phone jammed with voicemails. She saw that a large number of them came from Hoyt Wexford and Jon Aeppli, and she knew that she was going to have to call them before going to bed. She had smashed her knee into the side of the tanker when she boarded it, and was hit across the head and face with a pole by one of the tanker crew. She had also taken a couple of solid head and body shots while subduing the other crew members, but it was a far cry from falling from the height of the Statue of Liberty.

She collapsed in her bed in a state of utter exhaustion, promising herself she would recompose herself in a few minutes and make her calls to Hoyt and Jon. Only the extreme fatigue hit her like a ton of bricks, and she slipped into a deep, dreamless sleep which only reality would crash through on the following morning.

Chapter Seven

"This City has made a terrible blunder in refusing to pay the just tribute we deserve in sparing its people from devastation," the blurred figure of the Reaper was again broadcast around the world that Monday at noon on Eastern Standard Time. This time the video was uploaded onto You Tube, and a DVD copy sent by courier to City Hall. "Even worse is its pitiful recourse in turning to this Nightcrawler for protection. For these mistakes, the City of New York will be required to pay us ten times as much as we previously requested. We will now require one hundred million dollars to be paid as specified in order for us not to carry out our next attack. Twice you have seen how close you have come to unspeakable disaster. Twice you have narrowly escaped horrors unlike any ever known in the history of this nation. This time we will not fail to bring down a firestorm that will bring the State of New York to its knees. If we are not contacted with an offer to pay our fee, the people of New York will pay the ultimate price. We also intend to make a gruesome example of this Nightcrawler should he dare cross our paths again!"

"I thought we agreed you were not going back out, Bree," Jon Aeppli was exasperated when they met at the office Sunday morning. Jon told his wife he was meeting someone at the golf course, and Sabrina was forced to miss church once again. "That's a real beauty you picked up on your eye there. Are you gonna wear that balaclava of yours to meet Hoyt?"

"That's not funny, Jon," she scowled. She had a purple welt on her eye which had darkened her cheekbone from the pole that was smashed across her face on the previous day.

"Oh, I agree," he sat on the thick leather armchair by the plate glass window in her office. "So you say you took out twelve men? Did you gas them with the DATKO you agreed not to use anymore?"

"Gosh, I don't know, Jon, it all happened so fast," she laid back in her swivel chair behind her executive desk, staring at the ceiling, feeling as if she had been flattened by a steamroller. "I guess they heard the spear hit the side of the ship, and when I came over the side they all saw me. The one guy popped me with that pole and nearly knocked me out but I hit him with the gas. I tried to use as little as possible because of what you told me, and plus I didn't bring that much. I kinda used the gas gun as a weapon and took out a couple with that. I guess I was real lucky that they couldn't fight. Besides, they'd been drinking, and I really got the impression they weren't dead set on unloading the Agent BZ into the water. They saw all the people on the beach, and they must've known they would've been doing a terrible thing."

"And, of course, this wasn't anything the Coast Guard might've handled more efficiently."

"I'm sure you'd have to agree that the police would've never gotten to Pressley and De Lorean in time!" Sabrina insisted. "And I would've never got the information without the DATKO. You've got to realize that Al Qaeda, or whoever's backing the Octagon, must've paid them a ton of money. Maybe they didn't want to poison the water, but they sure as heck didn't want to give up their friends or associates either."

"So you're going to continue to take the risk of permanently disabling someone with the DATKO gas?"

"That's why I need your help, Jon. I can't do this all by myself, and everyone's turning their backs on me!" a tear ran down her cheek.

"I just want you to understand the ramifications of what you may be doing here," Jon said tautly. "The chemical weapons project was cancelled by the Government before your father died. If the product is ever traced back to our labs, we are going to be held liable on Federal charges. You stand to lose everything and might even be facing jail time, and that's not withstanding whatever they're willing to throw at you for your Nightcrawler routine. Are you still planning to continue with this?"

"I swear to you that if any of this comes back, I will never give you up and I will take full responsibility," she insisted. "You heard that maniac on the TV, he's planning to kill people. If they didn't give him ten million, he'll never get a hundred million, even if he learns how to bring fire from the sky. Just help me modify the DATKO and make it less toxic, that's all I ask."

"I suppose you'll need me to cover for you with Rod Ramirez as well. He called me to see whether that story of yours was on the up and up. I winged it the best I could, and it looks like he might be interested in picking up on that bogus dispersal agent deal you ran by him. I'll give you credit for one thing, you've got some imagination."

"I'm thinking if we can develop a compound that reduces the benzene toxicity in the weathered oil spill, we might be able to help Ramirez get a jump on the competition," she surmised. "He can bring that to the table with him when he negotiates his deals with the Mexican government, and that should help defray the cost of our research."

"Have you considered substituting toluene for the benzene in the dispersal compound?" Jon mused. "Toluene has a wider liquid range, plus there's less toxicity to have to deal with in the cleanup process."

"I'll give Ramirez a call and see what he thinks," she replied. "I just hope he hasn't put two and two together with that tanker bust."

"I think it would take a simpleton not to have figured that out, and I'm sure you've learned enough about Ramirez not to put him in that category," Jon rose to leave. "Now you've got me lying to my wife. Have fun explaining that shiner to Hoyt."

"Uh...I'll tell him you got mad about having to come in Sunday morning for no reason?"

"See you Monday," Jon walked out.

Sabrina took out her makeup kit and began studying her purple swelling while speed-dialing Hoyt on her cell phone.

"Bree," he sounded like he was outdoors. "I was just on my way to your house. I'm sure you heard the news by now. You know I got called out to help with the crowd control? I just can't believe what's happening. Are you okay? I've been trying to call you since yesterday afternoon."

"I'm so sorry," she did her best to sound apologetic, wincing as she daubed some foundation on her swollen temple. "I got all caught up in researching that asphalt compound we were working on, and I started looking at that fertilizer project, and the time just blew right by. I started driving around and by the time I got home I was just exhausted. I just met with Jon here at the office, and he was mad because he couldn't reach me yesterday. I hope you're not mad at me too."

"Someone with a voice as cute as yours is just too hard to get mad at. Can I meet you somewhere?"

"Sure can. Let's plan on an hour from now. I kinda got up on the wrong side of the bed this morning."

Sabrina came to work Monday morning with issues spilling off her plate. Tom Durham called back, saying the figures were solid and wanted to meet with Jon and Sabrina at Club 21 for lunch to sign the contracts and celebrate the deal. Her lawyer and CPA both called back and let her know that things were looking good with the adoption project. They suggested that Pastor Mitchell's own attorney and accountant give them a call to make sure no one missed anything. Rita Hunt had also called to let her know the pregnant girls were planning to meet at the church on Wednesday at the prayer service, and were looking forward to seeing Sabrina there.

CNN and the local news stations were reporting a rash of forest fires in the upstate New York area, rivaling that of the Manorville outbreak which consumed over a thousand acres in 2012. The fires had erupted in and around the Catskill Mountain range, and Homeland Security was concerned that this was not related to the Octagon terror threats. Sabrina also suspected that the Reaper may have launched this attack well ahead of time, setting it up in the secluded wilderness regions in case his attempts at the Statue of Liberty and Manhattan Beach failed.

Once again she was faced with the prospect of working this out without getting herself arrested in the process. In all likelihood, the chemically-proficient Octagon was using its expertise to initiate the brushfires. If she had a way to determine what kind of chemicals they were using, she might be able to obtain information as to who might have recently purchased similar items. Certainly the Reaper would not be so careless as to have a shipment of napalm or a related chemical weapon brought into the country. Yet he would more than likely have the means of mass-producing a hybrid fuel for an incendiary device.

As Sabrina began researching napalm products, she suddenly broke into a cold sweat in realizing that the benzene that she and Jon would be researching for Ramirez was an active ingredient in the napalm formula. She also saw that the polystyrene ingredient was a polymer derivative, which was also something they would be ordering for the Brooklyn Bridge project. Anyone in law enforcement who would be investigating chemical companies for possible involvement in the Octagon conspiracy would see red flags all over BCC's list of products to be ordered.

At once she was horrified to think that Ryan Hoffman might have something to do with it. If the Octagon was continuing to pressure him to assist them with their plans, he might easily have acted as the middle man in setting up a deal with a chemical supply company for the Reaper. She had been concerned with his sudden change in personality, even though he indicated he was dealing with the trauma of the failed blackmail attempt. It was highly possible that the Octagon was continuing to pressure him, and he might be up to his neck in whatever they were plotting now.

She decided to play her Hoyt card and give him a call. She was running out of people she could confide in without paying thousands of dollars for the privilege.

"I feel like I just hit the Lotto," Hoyt greeted her, the sound of outdoors coming over his cell phone. "Am I actually getting to talk to my little princess two days in a row?"

"I had something I needed to talk to you about. Do you think I could meet you at the River Café under the Brooklyn Bridge on the Brooklyn side? I've never been there. Dinner's on me."

"Maybe if it falls in your lap," he scoffed. "After work about four-thirty?"

"Kewl beans. See you then."

She next got Rita Hunt on the line, and both women were happy to hear from each other. She determined that she would set up some time to go out and socialize with Rita. She was pretty sure they would hit it off on a personal basis, and if she ever needed a friend it was now.

"Hey, Rita, my accountant's telling me I can get a $12,970 tax credit for helping out with this. The Pastor's not going to get anything out of it tax-wise since he's already has a tax-exempt status. Even so, that knocks the cost to a prospective couple down to around $17k. Maybe if you can do some surfing around the Internet and see if anyone's good with that price, I can try and set this up on my end."

"Gee, this sounds great," Rita was enthused. "If we can get Lindsay taken care of, maybe we can get a website going and get some donations for the other girls. If people read about Lindsay's story, they'll see how they can actually save a life through our program."

"That'd be wonderful. Say, I was wondering if you were busy tomorrow evening. I was thinking maybe I could come out and meet you, and we could grab a bite to eat. My friend Hoyt's a cop, and you can guess what weird hours he has. I get tired of eating by myself all the time, you know how that goes."

"Hey, I've been doing so much tuna fish I'm growing cat whiskers," Rita's laugh tinkled. "I'll cruise by the Church about five-ish tomorrow, sound okay?"

"See you then."

She realized she was going to have to deal with this situation with Ryan, but the worst thing would be to confront him directly. She decided that there had to be an indirect strategy in handling this, so her next move was to call Rick Alfonso in for a chit-chat.

"Hey, Sabrina, I hope you're not having boy trouble," Rick tried to be humorous, making a reference to the fading purple splotch over her right eye. He was a blond surfer type, a Brad Pitt lookalike with blue bedroom eyes and a captivating smile enhancing his slender, athletic build.

"Nah, nothing I can't handle," she replied cheerily. "I was just wondering where we were at with the Hunt proposal. Do we have any estimated figures yet?"

"I've got about three good bids coming in," he replied. "I'm just running through some red tape issues with the ammonium nitrate. With all the paranoia going around over those Octagon nut jobs, Homeland Security's checking out large orders everywhere. I was figuring I could expedite the arrangement by settling on a vendor, and then seeing if they could clear the order on their end before they ship to keep HS from crawling around over here."

"Darn it," Sabrina frowned. "Is Ryan having problems with the polymer? Are you guys ordering from the same places?"

"I'm not sure what he's got going. He hasn't been very talkative lately. I think he may be having some problems at home. It's kind of weird because normally he tells me everything. Let me touch bases with him and see what I can find out."

"Sounds good. If it's anything I need to know right away, you can call me on my cell."

"Is there something *I* should know?" Rick wondered. "This just sounds like run-of-the-mill red tape malarkey to me."

"I just wouldn't want them poking around here just when we're getting things back on track with these big contracts," she reassured him. "You know that if some of our prospects think we may be experiencing delays they might take their business elsewhere."

"Gotcha," Rick stood up to leave. "You better tell that guy of yours to lighten up on my sweetheart."

"Oh, I got him covered, don't worry about it," she giggled as Rick sashayed off.

She next sent an e-mail to Jon, Rick and Ryan congratulating them for the Company's achievement in landing the Durham contract. She also encouraged them to help her get the necessary estimates and overviews ready by Friday for her follow-up meeting with Durham. That would be a subtle nudge for Ryan so she could see what he was up to without prying into his activities. She then called the River Café to make reservations for her and Hoyt before getting ready to ride over the Club 21 with Jon to meet with Tom Durham for the contract signing.

Tom was in a cheery mood, and she had to endure a few minutes of good-natured ribbing after Durham saw the purple bruise on her eye that the makeup could not cover up. Jon was at a loss for words as Durham filled him in on all the details that Sabrina had left out about their workout session last week. He found it hard to believe that she hit Tom so hard in the solar plexus that he nearly called a timeout. Even harder to believe was him saying she was tougher than most of the men he had sparred with.

"I had one guy who was pretty sore about getting outbid on this deal," Durham knocked down a shot of Spanish brandy in a toast with them before signing the contracts. "I told him if he didn't like it, I'd put him in a room with the little girl who got it, and she'd beat the hell outta him."

Sabrina told Hoyt all about it a couple of hours later as they met under the Brooklyn Bridge and walked over by the fenceline overlooking the East River before heading into the River Café for dinner. He winced at the purple welt alongside her face, and she gave him some excuse about something falling from a shelf at the lab. Regardless of the bruise, he could not help but marvel at her lovely profile against the majestic New York skyline across the River. The sunlight played across her auburn hair and gave a sparkle to her emerald eyes, her upturned nose impish as she gave him a Cupid's-bow smile.

"I was kinda wondering if you might be able to do me a favor," she asked softly. "I want you to think about it carefully, and if it's out of the question I understand."

"Whatcha got?"

"I think someone's trying to set up BCC, to make us look bad. We're ordering some potentially volatile materials for some experiments we need for some of the projects I told you about. I'm afraid someone might try to get us red-flagged to slow us down and make our clients go elsewhere."

"How can I help?"

"I'd like to know what the investigators are coming across upstate, whether they're finding traces of chemicals that might have started the fires. If it's a case of arson, maybe I can find out what they're using and delay orders of those types of products. I can even look for alternative items so as not to disrupt our research."

"Why, sure, Bree. As a matter of fact, I'm sure anything you come across would help our guys upstate. I know a couple of guys up in Catskill, I'll give them a call and see if there's anything they can pass along."

"Great. Let's go inside, I'm starved."

"Hold on. Can I look at that?"

He wanted to wait until they left, but could not hold back any longer. He reached over and cupped her face in his hands, gazing into her eyes before slowly leaning forward and kissing her lips. Her heart fluttered as she closed her eyes and cherished the magic moment.

"Gosh, Hoyt," she caught her breath, "I—"

"Geez, I'm sorry, Bree—"

"Come on, silly," she took him hand and tugged him along. "Let's eat."

They got a table by the window and enjoyed a panoramic view of the New York harbor as they ordered their meals. Sabrina had the Maine lobster special while Hoyt tried the American red snapper. Hoyt splurged on the $100 three-course special, deciding that his first kiss from Sabrina was worth celebrating. They did not discuss the terrorists again, instead talking about places they had visited and how much fun it might be taking a run out of town to go sightseeing. Sabrina had not been to Disney World since she was a child, and they agreed that would be a great place to go one weekend.

They left as the sun went down, and Hoyt gave her a peck on the lips after walking her to her car, not wanting to embarrass her with people getting into a vehicle parked nearby. She exchanged hugs with him, and just as Hoyt walked off she got a call on her cell phone from Rick Alfonso.

"Bree? I was doing some checking around to try and get a handle on some of the stuff you were talking about. I got a call back from Rod Ramirez and he mentioned there was something you might find interesting. There's a firm called Anguiano Oil Exports operating out of Corpus Christi that has been moving barrels of oil to a location in Garrison, New York. I checked around and found that it's a warehouse that's been vacant for quite some time. Were you looking at Anguiano Exports for some reason? I'll be glad to check further if you like."

"No, no, that'll be fine," Sabrina replied softly. "I'll call Rod. Thanks a bunch."

It was a ninety-minute drive to Garrison from Staten Island, and she would need to go back home and pick up her gear before taking the drive. She knew that she might be able to crack this case if she drove up and investigated it herself. If she tipped off the cops, it was highly likely that the Octagon would have sentries posted if they were behind the scheme. They probably already had an alibi, and if the cops failed to take them down then they would move the petroleum to a safer and more secluded location.

It was almost ten that evening by the time she reached the outskirts of Garrison. She used her GPS to locate the warehouse, and stopped at a gas station to prepare for the ride out. She began feeling her stomach and legs cramping slightly and realized she was about to have her period. She cursed her luck and considered calling it off, but she had driven too far and had too much at stake to back off now. She smiled wryly as she considered what a rough time policewomen must have, and was glad she was only doing this on rare occasions.

She changed into her ninja suit in the restroom, putting her dress suit in her travel bag. Nobody even noticed as she had pinned her hair back and scrubbed her makeup off to appear less noticeable to busybodies. She hopped into the Porsche and headed north on IH-87 over the Palisades Interstate Parkway en route to Highway 9. The backroads were poorly illuminated and she had to stop and verify her GPS coordinates before parking her car at the deserted truck terminal. She saw the three-story warehouse building about a hundred yards off the side road and knew she had reached her destination.

She snuck up to the warehouse and saw a vehicle parked in the rear of the building, though there were no signs of movement anywhere. She checked the sliding steel door to the loading dock and found it locked. She went over to the glass-paned door leading to the side office and pried it open with her crowbar, stepping into the darkened room. There was a second door leading to the warehouse, and she found it unlocked as she slipped through. The barren room was about twenty square yards in area, and the only illumination came from the full moon shining brightly through the ceiling windows. She saw a metal staircase leading to an upper floor, and quickly tiptoed up the steps to see if there was anything hidden there.

She opened the door to the upper floor and the odor of petroleum hit her nostrils. She stepped into the moonlit room and saw about thirty oil barrels lining the far walls of the dark room. The walls featured large paned windows that provided for low visibility as she crept towards the center of the room.

"At last we meet," a voice thundered across the room as the fluorescent overhead lights flashed on. Sabrina shielded her eyes from the sudden brightness. She looked up and saw a tall, powerfully-built man walking towards the center of the room who she knew was the Reaper. To each side of him were two veiled figures, and on either side of them were two black-clad men carrying plexiglass riot shields. "It seems that all things come to those who wait, even Nightcrawlers."

"You know what they say about people who play with matches," she said, her voice distorted to a genderless growl by the device in her balaclava. "I've got the State Police arriving any minute now. I suggest you come on downstairs and give it up. If this turns into a shootout and one of these barrels explode, you people will be boiled alive."

"There's no one coming," the Reaper laughed as the two men circled around from either side of the room, shields at the ready. "The police are looking for you almost as hard as they're looking for us. You may have gotten in our way before but rest assured it will not happen again."

She pulled her gas gun and fired it at the attacker to her left as he brought his shield up to block the cloud of DATKO before it hit him. She whirled and fired a back kick to the shield of the second attacker, sending him flying backwards across the room. The first man slammed the shield against her arm, knocking the gas gun flying before she pirouetted and knocked him senseless with a roundhouse kick.

The Reaper moved across the floor like a jungle cat, launching himself through the air with a flying front kick that caught her in the left shoulder and sent her crashing against the wall. She started to rebound but was at once hit with a stomach cramp that felt like her tummy had been stapled. She broke into a defensive stance but was beset by the Reaper, who hit her with a volley of kicks and punches that left her out on her feet.

"This is just a question of having the right opponent in the right situation," the Reaper called back to his teammates as he stepped back defensively. "A bunch of useless Syrians were obviously no match for this one."

He then stepped it with a brutal right cross that sent her reeling backwards into the wall where she fell to her knees. The Reaper then kicked her in the head with his steel-tipped boot, dropping her flat on her face.

"You see how it is with these people who watch too many movies and think they can take the law into their own hands," the Reaper shook his head before grabbing her by the back of her collar and her belt, hoisting her up and throwing her onto a work table about ten feet away. "These stupid people think they can stick their nose into things that even Homeland Security can't handle!"

She felt the cramps doubling up as if she had been kicked in the stomach. She was still seeing double from the kick to the head and doubted she would be able to block him again, much less fight back. She had a knife in her rucksack but would not be able to reach it before he made his next move. She was in serious trouble, and realized she was just about out of options as the Reaper drew near.

"Let us take a look at this fool before we finish him off," the Reaper chortled, grabbing her balaclava. "I think we'll leave him outside for the police after we get these barrels loaded up."

Sabrina reached up and grabbed his wrist but was unable to stop him from tearing the hood from her head.

"What in hell is this?" the Reaper exclaimed. "This is not the Nightcrawler. This is a girl!"

"Obviously this must be a group going under the guise of the Nightcrawler," the Tarantula came over to where the Reaper stood by the table. "This is not going to end the problem."

"She's very pretty," Vincent Gargano observed as he drew near. The eyes of the bisexuals narrowed with lust as they were aroused by the vicious beating. "Let us have some fun with her first."

"You know," the Reaper stared him down, "your proclivities can be offensive at times."

With that, he grabbed her by the front of her jacket and her belt buckle. He swung her off the table in a short arc, and threw her through the air crashing out the paned window where she plummeted almost thirty feet to the ground below.

Chapter Eight

The next day, the Governor of New York called out the National Guard. They set a blockade around the forest fire to prevent anyone from accessing the area. The State Police and SWAT units raided the Garrison warehouse just before daybreak and confiscated the petroleum barrels though the Octagon had long since departed. They fled the scene immediately upon discovering the Nightcrawler had vanished.

Hoyt Wexford had followed a hunch and staked out Sabrina's home after they left the River Café Monday evening. He waited outside for about an hour until she left the manor in her Porsche, accessing the Verrazano-Narrows Bridge and heading north towards IH-87. He followed her carefully towards Garrison, watching and waiting as she entered the gas station wearing her dress suit and exiting in a black martial arts uniform. He felt his bowels churning as she drove a short distance to Highway 9 where she came to a halt and parked at the deserted warehouse.

He parked in the bushes alongside the road and crept onto the warehouse property, his heart filled with trepidation. He was almost sickened by the thought of her masquerading as the Nightcrawler, and wondered what would make her go to such extremes to uncover a suspected plot against her Company. He saw a truck parked in the back and assumed that someone had agreed to meet her out here. He only hoped that it was someone who had access to the property and that neither were trespassing or breaking into the building.

His heart sank as he saw her breaking into the warehouse, and wrestled with the notion of taking off so as not to be accused of witnessing the crime. Yet he would not leave this beautiful girl he was falling in love with, and decided to stick around until she came back out. He would let her see his vehicle leave the area and let her do some serious thinking about someone having seen her on the premises.

He received the shock of his life when she came crashing out the window, bumping and rolling in a heap on the grass twenty yards in front of him. He drew his gun and waited as a figure looked out the window at her before the lights went out once more. He waited a couple of minutes before darting from the bushes, picking her up in his arms and carrying her away. He had no idea of how many people were in the building and what he would be up against if he tried to take them on. If he called for backup, Sabrina would be in deep stuff if they connected her to the Nightcrawler or found she had broken into the building.

"Hoyt?" she managed weakly, trying to remain conscious as he loaded her into the back seat of his midnight blue BMW. "Don't go in there, there's too many of them."

"I've got to get you to a doctor," he insisted as he hopped into the driver's seat and gunned the engine.

"No! Don't you do it!" she gasped in pain. "You either get us a room or just leave me here. No cops, no doctors!"

"All right, I'll get us a room and check you out. If you need to be in a hospital, you're going," he admonished her.

He drove a short distance along the IH-87 South and pulled into a motel run by an East Indian. He winced at the curry smell that permeated the office, paying with his credit card before getting the key and driving to the rear of the property. He opened up the door and carried Sabrina inside, laying her gently on one of the double beds.

"We need to get my car over here," she said weakly.

"Baby, you're all wet. Is that blood?" he stared at her pants.

"I just started my period and that goofball threw me out the window," she grunted. "Help me to the bathroom so I can get cleaned up. Why don't you call a cab and get my car while you're waiting?"

"Okay," he agreed as she pulled her keys from her pocket and tossed them to him. He then came over and she struggled to her feet as he put his arm around her and walked her to the bathroom. He was nearly overwhelmed by concern for her, anger at what had been done to her, and the feel of her voluptuous figure in his arms. Even though he was handling her as the most fragile crystal, she was still the sexiest woman alive for him. He could not believe they were together this intimately in such a terrible situation.

"Oh, and can you stop somewhere and get me some tampons, and some aspirin?" she called before closing the bathroom door.

"Yeah, sure," he was on his way out to the car.

"And some iron pills, and milk, and a hamburger if you see one."

"Yes, ma'am," he managed a chuckle, suspecting that she was somehow regaining her strength. He was filled with gladness, yet resolved that he was going to get to the bottom of this.

He would find out how in hell she ended up getting thrown out of that window.

She had sufficiently recovered to make the drive home the next morning before dawn, and Hoyt gave her enough time before calling the State Police. She called Jon Aeppli and told him she was taking the day off before arriving at the manor and nearly crawling from the garage to the house. She had the car radio on throughout the drive, but the news about the Guard was not broadcast until 8 AM. *Good Morning America* announced that a break in the Octagon case had resulted in a warehouse stacked with petroleum barrels having been raided. They also reported that the Governor had been notified, and he was deploying the Guard to the Catskills.

Miraculously, she managed to do a parachutist roll when she hit the grass outside the warehouse. She landed on both feet and rolled backwards, though she hit hard on her back and was sent sprawling onto her head and neck. She was sore from the fall, her face swollen and even more mottled by the head shots she took from the Reaper. To add insult to injury, this was all happening at this time of the month. She had cramps, a double headache, and felt like hunting down the Octagon and pulling their hair out.

Of all the things that weren't going to happen today, canceling supper with Rita was going to be the worst. She was really looking forward to spending some quality time with Rita and hopefully find the unmet friend. When she looked back on her life, most of her friends were what she considered periodic friends. They were the ones who were there for the season, then disappeared from her life. There were the pre-school friends, the grade school friends, the high school friends, those from NYU and the ones from John Jay. She could count her close friends on one hand, and hoped Rita would be a keeper. Hopefully she would be ambulatory enough to meet with Rita on Friday. The only thing that would keep her from making it would be getting thrown out another window.

Tomorrow was the Church meeting with the expectant mothers, and there was no way she was missing that. She would reschedule with Rita while firming up the Wednesday appointment. She would make that even if she had to walk in on crutches. Her only dread was that the Pastor saw her like that, and put two and two together. He would realize she went Nightcrawling, and he would jump on the bandwagon to make her quit. After the whipping she took from the Reaper, she did not think it would take a lot to make her change her mind.

She bared her soul at the motel last night, and he sat spellbound as she told him all about the Nightcrawler. He was very quiet as she gave all the details of the last couple of months, and they were both very tired by the time she finished. He left a wake-up call for five AM, and they woke the next morning engrossed in thought over the things they had to attend to this day. He hugged and kissed her but it was not with the passion of yesterday at the River Café. She hoped she had not lost him, but even more important, she prayed he would not betray her.

She began crying as she thought of how she was beginning to feel about Hoyt. He was strong, level-headed and devoted, the kind of guy every girl was looking for. Only his career meant everything to him at this stage of his life. He had just graduated from the Academy and was already getting choice assignments. He was ending up in the thick of major events, and the people on top were beginning to take notice. She did not want the Nightcrawler to come between them, and even worse, she did not want the Nightcrawler to put her in a wheelchair or a casket.

Only she could not feel a sense of pride in what the Nightcrawler had accomplished. She had stopped the Octagon three times in a row, and saved New York from disaster at least twice. There would have been no way the police could have captured the petroleum barrels if it were not for the Nightcrawler. Yet she was astonished by the fact that they were still looking for the Nightcrawler for possession of chemical weapons. It was almost as if everyone wanted for her to abandon an alter ego that had saved so many innocent lives.

It was the call from Rod Ramirez that turned her day topsy-turvy. She was not going to pick up at first, but realized that it was his tipoff to Rick Alfonso that made the Garrison gambit happen. She was apprehensive over the fact that he now had some serious weight on her, but she was also sure that he did not want to get caught up an investigation if the Feds tried to link the BCC up to Laredo Oil and Gas. Plus she did not want to do anything to show disrespect.

"Hi, Mr. Ramirez, how are you today?" Sabrina sounded cheery.

"Just fine, my dear. I wanted you to be among the first to know that I have retired to Southern Mexico."

"What?" she was perplexed.

"A lot has happened over the past few days, my dear," he seemed apologetic. "A lot of things that I have come to regret. Obviously things have worked out for the best, but I fear I will spend many sleepless nights thinking of how it all could have gone the other way."

"What kind of things?" she tried to get up from her recliner in the living room but it hurt too much.

"Somehow Al Qaeda found out about how you traced that oil tanker from El Paso to New York," he revealed. "They gave me a take-it-or-leave-it proposition, an ultimatum, if you will. They asked me to help entice you to send the Nightcrawler to investigate their storage depot in Garrison. Somehow they compromised my connection in Nuevo Laredo to divulge my involvement in discovering the rogue tanker. They offered to buy my company for ten million dollars and the chance to walk away with my life."

"My gosh, Mr. Ramirez, they nearly killed me," she said softly.

"I was fairly certain you would notify the police as you did at Manhattan Beach," he insisted. "I did not think you would be foolish enough to try and take them on by yourself."

"That's not how it went down at Manhattan Beach," a tear of anger rolled down her cheek. "That's what the papers said, but that's not what happened."

"Well, you are safe now, that is what matters," he rationalized. "I just felt that the information I gave them along with my business was worth more than their equivalent of thirty pieces of silver. They told me they would kill me if they ever heard from me again. So, now I tell you what they did not think was worth paying for."

"And what's that?" she asked intently.

"I'm pretty sure I know what the Octagon's Plan B is."

The following morning, Sabrina returned to work and joined the rest of the staff at the Brooks Chemical Company to watch another *Good Morning America* exclusive. Undercover officer Hoyt Wexford had received a tip that helped police uncover over a thousand barrels of petroleum stored in an abandoned mine in the Catskills. The barrels had been rigged with C4 plastic explosives that would have started a firestorm high in the mountain area unreachable by firefighting units.

Sabrina tried calling Hoyt but his phone immediately went to voicemail. She was exceedingly happy for him and glad she was able to keep the Nightcrawler out of it. She called him as soon as she got off the phone with Ramirez and told him of the information she was given. It was Ramirez's measure of revenge for them having squeezed him out of a business he had devoted his working life to. The business itself was worth over $100 million, but Ramirez had invested so heavily that after liquidation, he might have been lucky to walk away with the ten million Al Qaeda gave him. Still, if he had been able to hang in for ten more years, he would have easily retired with fifty million. Asking for twenty million was not unreasonable, and when they spit in his face, he spit back.

What shook her to the core was an exclusive news bulletin by CNN that afternoon. Vincent Gargano and Walt Griffin were arrested shortly after the Homeland Security raid, and they both maintained that they had been blackmailed into the Octagon by an extortion ring led by the Nightcrawler. They said that they were just one of several people in the LGBT community that had been approached by the ring. They had been forced to divulge professional secrets and personal identity info of others under threat of having their own private information exposed. In their case, they had been forced to join the Octagon for what they were told was a project for a private overseas security agency. It was rumored that the ACLU was planning to represent the men, who were also being championed by the LGBT community.

"This is a perfect example of why this Administration needs to step in and eliminate sexual discrimination from our society once and for all," LGBT activist Sheryl Harrington was interviewed on CNN. Harrington was a transsexual standing six feet tall with one hundred eighty five pounds set on an athletic frame. "Members of our community should no longer be forced to hide in closets for fear of being ostracized over their sexual identities. The LGBT community has been lobbying to have sexual discrimination against gays categorized as hate crimes. Issues such as these should cause our legislators to wake up and realize how this social injustice is threatening the safety and security of our very nation!"

Sabrina sat in her office trying to absorb the impact of what she had seen and heard when the phone rang. She glanced at her Caller ID and was relieved to see it was Rita.

"Hi, honey," her Kentuckian drawl was chipper as always. "Just checking to see if you were still gonna make the prayer meeting tonight. We were also gonna discuss plans for a barbecue event on the Church property to benefit the women's shelter project. We were thinking about holding it this Saturday, and I wasn't sure if you knew about it because it had just come up over the last couple of weeks.

"

"Why, that sounds like a great idea!" Sabrina snapped out of her funk. "I'm heading straight over there after I get home from work. See you then."

Jon Aeppli came to her office after lunch, having spent most of the morning with Rick Alfonso and Tom Durham making plans for the Brooklyn Bridge project. He seemed very distracted and Sabrina settled in her desk for what she was sure would be a long sermon.

"I just don't know what to say," he lowered his head as he rested his elbows on the arms of the overstuffed chair before her desk. "It just seems like you can't win for losing with this little enterprise of yours. I see you're limping again, doubtlessly over what I'm sure was another one of your escapades. Now you've got the LGBT people howling for the Nightcrawler's blood again. When is this all going to end?"

"Now, Jon, I'm sure you got all riled up over watching TV this morning. I'm sure you must've seen something about Hoyt uncovering an Octagon plot to blow up an entire section of the Catskills mountain range. He might come out with a Medal of Valor for this. Considering all that we've accomplished, I don't think a little mudslinging by the LGBTers should invalidate everything else."

"Did you also know that Rod Ramirez closed his place down this weekend?" he studied her face carefully.

"Uh, he called me yesterday and mentioned it."

"Don't you think it was a little bit more than a coincidence?"

"You may be right. Being so close to the Gulf of Mexico and with all those out-of-country connections, he might have got involved in some bad business."

"And, of course, there's no chance of us being implicated in anything like that."

"That's why I asked you and Rick to reach out to our suppliers to make sure we weren't going to get red-flagged by Homeland Security if we start placing those new orders," she insisted. "I've already given you my word. I'm not going to let my crime prevention endeavors compromise the future of this company."

"Okay, so you've built this dichotomy for yourself that won't allow you to listen to reason," Jon got up, heading out the door. "I'm not worried about the Company, Sabrina. I'm worried about you."

"I'll be all right," she said in a small voice.

"You've got so much to live for, kid," he said ruefully, patting the doorframe before returning to his office.

The rest of the day was fairly uneventful save for a couple of calls from James Hunt, looking to secure a start date for discussions on his upcoming project. Sabrina opted for next Friday, which would make it a leisurely bull session providing for a full-throttle start on the following Monday. She sent e-mails to Jon and Ryan, informing them of the power lunch before taking off at four-thirty that afternoon.

She drove home and took a shower, washing off some of the Ben-Gay and changing to a pants suit before heading back out to the Staten Island Ferry and taking the boat over to Lower Manhattan. She reached the Church shortly before six PM, greeting Rita and the other girls before Pastor Mitchell arrived.

"I'm afraid I've got some bad news about the barbecue this Saturday afternoon," the Pastor was disconsolate. "The City denied us the permits we needed to extend the event past our property lines. There seemed to be a protest from the LGBT community over the purpose of the activity. I was also given a friendly word of advice that we might want to postpone this indefinitely until the political atmosphere improves."

"What on earth could those people be on about now?" Sabrina was exasperated, still smarting over the backlash against the Nightcrawler on TV earlier that day.

"They feel that our religious convictions may be discriminatory as far as restricting their community's right to adopt," he said sadly. "I think we've got a good legal foundation when push comes to shove, but at this stage things could get hairy if they start demonstrating against us."

"We can't back down now, we've sent out too many invitations!" Rita objected. "We've got some influential people who've visited our website and are very supportive of our cause. They've committed to coming down and making donations, and we just stand to lose too much if we cancel the event."

"We can have it at my house," Sabrina spoke up. "I'm about ten minutes from the ferry station. If they use Google or Map Quest, it'll put them right on my doorstep. I've got a big back yard with a fence, we'll have privacy and all the room we need, plus plenty of parking. I think I'll even get us a couple of those big barbecue cookers and some extra meat, since everybody's gonna be taking the ferry boat ride out to see us."

"Are you sure it won't be too much trouble?" the Pastor was hesitant.

"There's nothing I can do for God that I'd consider too much trouble," she said merrily.

"Well, I certainly can't argue with that," Mitchell was somewhat relieved. "I guess I'll let you and Rita work out the details and make sure everyone knows about the change in plans."

"Sounds fantastic," Rita was delighted as the young women all thanked Sabrina for her kindness.

"Uh, Sabrina—?"

"Yes, Pastor?"

"Do you think I could have a word after the meeting?"

Hoyt called when she got home, and he was still in Garrison meeting with Homeland Security over the recent incident. They put him up in a local hotel, and he was ecstatic over the prospect of being nominated for a Medal of Valor. Only he was enervated from all the tension-filled activity and could not wait to see Sabrina again.

"They were grilling me hard over the Nightcrawler," he admitted. "They couldn't believe I got a tip like that from an anonymous caller, especially after the first one about the warehouse. I'll wait until I see you to tell you more about it. I don't want to get into it on a hotel telephone."

"Okay," she was in her oval bed in her large and comfortable bedroom at the manor, clad in her silk pajamas. "You better make sure you invite me to that award ceremony when you get that medal, or I'm gonna be pretty upset."

"Are you kidding? If you don't show up, I'm not going."

"Well, then, we've got a date. You're coming out to my place for the barbecue Saturday, right?"

"If you're there, I wouldn't miss it for the world."

"Call me when you get in?"

"Don't bet against it."

They gave each other big loud smooches over the phone before hanging up, and Sabrina fell asleep feeling like a teenager in love.

He returned to town Friday evening, and they met for dinner that night before taking a carriage ride around Central Park. She rode with her head on his shoulder and his arm around hers, and she could not think of a time when she had been happier. She only hoped that his recent achievements would earn him a desk job somewhere so she wouldn't have to worry about him taking risks out on the field in future.

She woke up bright and early the next morning and hired some of the landscapers at BCC to come out and help set up for the barbecue. Her father had a stack of folding tables and chairs in one of the garage areas for such occasions, and she called a rental place to bring out some large barrels and mobile pits for the set-up. She next had a couple of slabs of beef and cafeteria-sized salad containers delivered, expecting as many as one hundred people who responded to Rita's website invitation. As an afterthought, she even rented a couple of Port-O-Sans.

The guests started arriving about ten AM for the event, but Sabrina also noticed cars parking in a field down the way from them where people began congregating. The crowd outside was much smaller than that out on her lawn, but continued growing nonetheless. Eventually they began moving closer and closer to her front gates until they were standing directly across the street.

"My goodness," Pastor Mitchell came over to where Sabrina was standing at the gate entrance to the manor. They were astonished at the sight of television broadcast vehicles pulling up along the side street. "I can't believe those people would go to this extreme."

They were chagrined as the news reporters attempted to interview some of the expectant mothers as they made their way up to Sabrina's home. Some of them wiped away tears as they were asked personal questions about their pregnancies and personal situations. More than a few of the benefactors and invitees had choice words for the reporters and protestors as they continued to beleaguer the woman attending the barbecue.

"This kind of discrimination not only violates gay rights, but compromises the future of these innocent children!" Al Carbone, a 6'4", 300-pound man wearing a wig and summer dress, thundered into a microphone before the cameras. "My partner is a professional earning over one hundred thousand dollars per year, and could provide a child nearly three times the benefits of a lower middle-class Christian family. I also know of business associates of mine who earn twice as much as my partner does. What right do these Christians have to pick and choose who has a chance at a better life than another child?"

Sabrina was beside herself as she called Hoyt to see if there was anything that could be done. He put her on hold and made a couple of calls, and was told that the LGBT demonstrators were perfectly within their rights as long as they were not on Sabrina's property.

"Don't worry, sweetheart," he assured her. "Go on and get back to your party. I'll be there in a little bit, and we'll see what's what."

Sabrina remained the perfect hostess, going from table to table to meet and greet everyone and make sure all the guests had plenty to eat. She recognized more than a few people from Chamber of Commerce meetings she had attended, and took occasion to exchange business cards and schedule some power lunches.

Everyone was surprised as a number of patrol cars pulled up in front of the manor gates. Sabrina rushed over to see what was happening, and was surprised to see Hoyt emerging from the lead vehicle.

"Hi, baby," he pecked her on the cheek, clad in a white silk shirt and jeans in the mild June weather. "Hope I'm not late."

"What's going on?" she wondered.

"I just thought I'd have some friends come out and check out some of your barbecue," he said airily. She watched as over a dozen gay cops climbed out of their vehicles, going directly over to the crowd of demonstrators to exchange words. The LGBT protestors started to argue but saw they had been trumped by Hoyt's gambit.

"You better get down from that fence, baby, or you're gonna get hurt," a black cop lisped angrily at a man who had climbed up on Sabrina's gate.

"I'm demonstrating for gay rights!" the man insisted.

"I'm gonna give you some gay rights and lefts if you don't get down!" the cop snapped at him.

"Oh, Hoyt, what a wonderful surprise," Sabrina hugged him.

"Well, you owe me, lady," he winked at her. "I'm going over to where they're cutting on that slab of beef and get some payback."

Sabrina saw a couple of people from the group of protestors coming through the gate, and headed over to make sure this was not going to get out of hand.

"Excuse me, Miss Brooks," one of the two women spoke up, both considerably larger in size than Sabrina. Upon closer inspection she could see that they were transgendered. "My name is Callen Marlowe, I'm a reporter from *Gay Garden* magazine. I was noticing what a lovely garden and landscape you have along the sides of the house and was wondering if I could take some pictures. We haven't done any features on this side of the Island for a while, and thought your home would be a great place to start. Plus, maybe if these people saw us walking around, they might consider calling it a day."

"Sure, why not?" Sabrina agreed. "Go right ahead. Here's my business card, just give me a call if anyone wants to come back out. You can get yourselves some food if you like."

Sabrina returned to the party as the solidly-built women strolled towards the rear of the house with their equipment bags in tow. They took pictures and looked around, nonchalantly peeking through windows until they found what they were looking for.

"Here we go," said Sheryl Harrington as she located the master bedroom. Callen opened the largest bag and pulled out a large flowerpot containing some fresh sprouts. She set the pot slightly behind a bed of roses right beneath the bedroom window.

"Hello?" a muffled voice answered a cell phone.

"This is the Tarantula," Callen replied. "Mission accomplished."

"Excellent," the Reaper replied. "Better get out of there so no one gets a chance to remember what you looked like."

The women furtively exited through the main gate, feeling triumphant in having made a move that they felt would end the threat of the Nightcrawler once and for all.

Chapter Nine

L.I. RESIDENTIAL EXPLOSION UNDER INVESTIGATION – HEIRESS' BODY MISSING

—(AP) A mysterious explosion at a Long Island residence early Sunday morning may have resulted in the death of the heiress of the Brooks Chemical Company. Sabrina Brooks, 24, was home at the time of the blast but her remains have yet to be found. The intensity of the explosion incinerated a large portion of the mansion, but police have not confirmed whether Ms. Brooks' body was rendered untraceable.

Ms. Brooks hosted a Church barbecue earlier in the day that sparked a sizeable protest over the non-denomination's pro-life adoption policies. Police are investigating whether the event may have triggered the attack.

Neighborhood Security kept an emergency list for everyone in the exclusive South Shore residential section, and contacted Jon Aeppli and Hoyt Wexford immediately after the blast was reported. They found each other after arriving to find firefighters working desperately to contain the two-alarm blaze.

"I can't believe this," Hoyt was in a state of distraction, tears spilling down his cheeks. "How could something like this happen?"

"I hope it didn't have anything to do with that trip you two took upstate," Jon said quietly.

"She told you about that?" Hoyt stared at him.

"I've known her all her life," Jon said, his eyes misty. "She trusted me with lots of things."

"Nightcrawler?"

"Yeah."

"I'm gonna get whoever did this. I swear I'll make them pay for this."

"That's exactly what she wouldn't want," Jon insisted. "She cared for you, kid, cared for you a lot. She wouldn't have wanted anything to happen to you. This should be enough. Please, for Sabrina's sake. Let the FBI and Homeland Security get those rats."

"I can't promise you anything," Hoyt managed. "I won't rest until they're caught, but I'll try to stay with the pack so I can see those slimeballs get taken down."

Jon drove home and could not even think of going back to bed. When he went to work, the entire hundred-person staff was in the lobby awaiting him. He told them what he had witnessed at her home, and they were in a state of distraction as they went about their duties.

"Good gosh, Jon, this is terrible," Rick Alfonso came to his office shortly afterwards. "Where are you gonna start with this? Do you have any contact information for her relatives? Did Vern ever mention anything about how the Company was going to be administered if anything happened to Sabrina?"

"I'm in the same boat as everyone else," Jon admitted. "I'm gonna call the family lawyer and see what he's got. As far as this place goes, I think it'll be best for us to keep things going as best we can until the lawyer lets us know where we stand on legal ground. Knowing Vern Brooks as well as I did, I'm pretty positive he had some contingency plan in case something like this ever happened."

As senior partners, Jon, Rick and Ryan stayed well past regular hours to make sure they contacted all their clients and let them know they were expecting a seamless transition as Sabrina's affairs were settled. The three of them refused to accept any calls, avoiding the press as they struggled through the day. They all stayed later than normal, though Jon was first to leave as he had been awake and under enormous stress since two-thirty that morning.

Rick Alfonso was feverishly at work at his desk on the Durham project. He knew that if Vern Brooks had made contingency plans to liquidate the company in the event of Sabrina's demise, then time was of the essence. It would take Vern's lawyer time to file all the legal paperwork and assume power as executor to release everyone from employment before beginning the liquidation process. Rick knew that if he could get some extra front money from Durham, their bonus clauses would kick in and they would all walk away from the table with a little extra.

He saw a figure walk into the room through the shadows, as he had cut off his fluorescent light and switched to his desk lamp as was Company policy. Vern Brooks established it as a signal to outsiders that the business was closed and personnel was burning the midnight oil. He continued researching his databases until a soft hand brushed his cheek.

"Working late again?"

"I think we all should

be," Rick muttered. "They're not exactly giving out golden parachutes when this place crashes and burns, you know."

"I just can't believe it's all come to this," Ryan Hoffman sighed forlornly as he stared out the picture window overlooking the fields covering the north end of the building. "Just last year, Vern was nearly doubling our projection figures, Sabrina was majoring in law enforcement, and it looked like we were going to be all going to retire here. How could it have come to this?"

"Life sucks, and then you die," Rick grumbled. "Things change, especially for gay people. Why do you think the Jews and the blacks treat us so well? They know just what it's like. Times and opinions can change in the blink of an eye. One minute you're on top, and the next minute when things go bad, they're looking for scapegoats. If they sell this place and some macho straight guy takes over, we'll probably be the first to get our pink slips. I say we just milk this cow and get the heck out of Dodge."

"What about *us*, Rick?" Ryan insisted, his voice quivering. "I thought we had something going between us. I know we haven't been…together in a long time, but that doesn't change what I feel for you."

"My feeling have never changed for you either, you know that," Rick kept his eyes glued to his PC monitor as he typed in data. "We both know it was too risky to keep it going. My wife was suspicious about me coming home late all the time and so was yours. She's going to be on me like flies on poop when I get home tonight. We've got too much to lose by having an affair, we've talked about this time and again. I think we need to focus more on keeping what we got than wishing for what might never be. We need to start on trying to keep this place open for at least a few more paydays."

"I love you, Rick," Ryan wiped his eyes.

"Love you too," he replied. "Go on home and get some sleep. We've got a long day ahead of us tomorrow."

He waited until he heard the door from Ryan's office close, then the heavy metal exit door on the side of the silent building. He listened for Ryan's car to start up, and the gravel crunching under his tires as he finally took off for home. Rick then got up and went over to Sabrina's office, switching on her PC and logging in under her 'guest' password that she stupidly never bothered to convert.

It was the whole family business concept that was Vern Brooks' downfall, If he would have set everything up so that Jon Aeppli would have benefitted from a Brooks tragedy, this scenario would have never happened. Everyone knew that Sabrina was just a spoiled little airhead who didn't have the discipline or the character to follow in her father's footsteps. Vern was a hunk who Rick would have gone down on in a New York minute. His daughter was the exact opposite: a weak, unfocused little party girl spending money faster than she could ever make it. This ship was destined to sink and Rick was the only one smart enough to grab a life raft.

When Sheryl and Callen reached out to him back around springtime, he put them on hold for fear of being discovered by Vern and risking termination and possible imprisonment. When Vern met his untimely demise, it seemed as if an omen that would change his life. He called the girls back and told them the deal was a go. He also found that his incredible streak of luck continued as Sabrina had not changed her password. He was able to hack into the classified database and access all the information from the military project. Jon Aeppli continued thinking it was Sabrina opening the database from her workstation as Rick turned all the chemical weapon research files over to Sheryl and Callen for five hundred thousand dollars.

The Octagon's scam was a stroke of genius. They had already been paid $100 million by Al Qaeda to launch a chemical attack on New York City. Regardless of whether they succeeded or not, it would lock down the Empire State in a red alert state of emergency for another ten years. The Reaper's demands for extortion money was just a ruse, weakening the citizens' resolve in making them second-guess the prevailing philosophy to never meet terrorists' demands. When they released the Kolokol-1 over the East River during the upcoming Fourth of July celebration, nearly one million people would be injured or killed by the gas. Al Qaeda would announce that they paid the Octagon five hundred million dollars for completing the attack. It would leave the people of New York, and the world, forever wondering why their Government could not have spared the money to save so many lives.

"Good evening, Rick," he heard an electronic voice in the doorway that nearly made him jump out of his skin. "Looks like you lost your way back to your desk in the dark."

He looked up and saw a shadowy figure rush towards him, and he rose just as a cloud of a powdery substance seemed to engulf him. He felt as if he had been submerged underwater, his ears and throat clogged and his tongue thickened so as almost to gag him. He dropped back in the overstuffed swivel chair and tried to move his arms and legs to no avail.

"Your wife and kids are outside," a voice called to him from miles away. "If you don't tell me everything I want to know, I'm going to bring them in and make you confess you're a sissy."

"No—aaghh—" Rick was barely able to move his tongue.

"Mrs. Alfonso?" the voice called loudly from across the void.

"No—" he pleaded. "No—!"

"Okay, then. You better admit everything, just answer yes or no."

It seemed to Rick as if thirty years, but thirty minutes passed in real time before the unending torrent of questions abated. He was starting to regain movement, floundering around as if he had just been rescued from drowning. He felt as if he was roaring drunk, unable to remember from one minute to the next. He only knew that his wife and kids might have been sitting outside, and hopefully they would be able to drive him home once he was able to get up on his feet.

"*Sabrina!*"

Jon Aeppli had gotten home and realized that he left a finalized report on the Durham project on his desk. He had to drive back all the way from Bensonhurst to get it, as he had called Durham earlier that day and told him it would be ready for pickup tomorrow. He was stunned to see the light on in Sabrina's office, and even more so at what he discovered.

"Hi, Jon," she said meekly. "I caught Rick looking at stuff he shouldn't be looking at, and it sure's not porn. I think you should fire him."

"Oh, Sabrina," Jon rushed over and took her in his arms, hugging her tight. "Why didn't you at least call me? I was at your house last night with Hoyt, it was the most terrible night of my life. We thought you had been burned alive."

"I just took the opportunity to check on some stuff," she said apologetically. "I wouldn't have caught this rat messing with my computer if he thought I was still around. He set Ryan up, and he sold all our classified WMD research to the Octagon."

"I'm calling the police," Jon reached into his pocket for his cell phone.

"No, don't," she pleaded. "Just let him go. He'll be sorry. He's been here for years, and now he won't dare even use us for a reference. I'm sure his wife and kids have been through enough already."

"What are you gonna do now?" he asked, marveling at her Nightcrawler uniform with the balaclava draped around her neck. "You look like a mutant ninja turtle."

"I've got to figure out what the Octagon's gonna do with those formulas. Al Qaeda's not shipping the WMD's in, they're making the chemical ingredients available through the black market. The Octagon ordered the chemicals weeks in advance, thanks to this tapeworm. The Russian Mob has already delivered the ingredients for Kolokol-1. They're planning a strike at the Fourth of July celebration on the East River. I just have to figure how they're planning on pulling it off."

"No!" Jon was adamant. "This is too big for you! You can't risk innocent lives by going at this on your own! If you fail or miscalculate, there'll be over a million people exposed to that gas!"

"Okay, reason with me," she insisted. "First of all, these guys got paid in advance. They're following through because they're trying to get in on the international level. I did my homework, I know who the Reaper is. He threw me out a window a few days ago. His name is Dalibor Branko, he was a leader with the Serbian Liberation Army in Kosovo in the 90's. He's wanted throughout Europe for war crimes, but Interpol thinks he's dead. He's connected with the Russian Mob, and they're the ones moving the chemicals for Al Qaeda. If he pulls this off, they'll send the Octagon back to Europe for operations against the European Union. He thinks I'm dead and no one else's close to catching him. He's got his money, he thinks he's out of here after this, he'll be careless and I'll nail him this time."

"No way, young lady. They've nearly killed you, I'm not standing by while you give them another chance."

"Follow your heart, Jon," Sabrina entreated him as she headed out the door. "You know I'm right, and you know I can get this guy. If you call the cops, they'll issue an alert and he'll dump it on the street or in the water. He has absolutely nothing to lose. I'm betting he's going to try and drop it during the air show. Once it's off the ground and I take him out, we can have the police capture the aircraft and move it over the ocean where it can't hurt anyone."

"It's too risky," he warned her. "I'm calling the cops."

"Follow your heart," she pleaded before disappearing down the hall.

He tapped the cell phone in his pocket, looking down at the semi-conscious figure of Rick Alfonso. Resisting an urge to kick him in the teeth, he resigned himself to sitting in Sabrina's chair and waiting for the renegade to come to his senses.

Hoyt Wexford had an early supper and caught a nap before heading out for a late shift that evening. Security was high for the upcoming Fourth of July holiday, and he was going to meet with his unit to discuss contingency operations in the event there was an emergency during the celebration. It would be a gratuitous appearance on his part as he was being decorated with the Medal of Valor in a ceremony next week. He was also being promoted to Sergeant and given a detective's badge. He had requested time off to recover himself after Sabrina's death, and the Department could not refuse such a celebrated member of the force. Yet they would require him to respond in case of emergency, so he would attend the meeting to receive instructions before taking his leave.

He climbed into his BMW and fumbled for his keys, nearly moved to tears by the thought of Sabrina. He realized now that he had fallen in love with her, and kicked himself for not having told her before she was killed. If they had been sleeping together, he might have saved her or at least died with her. He would never know what it would have been like to have held her body close to his, to have made love to her, to have seen her eyes when he proposed to her. He would never love another woman the way he loved her, and he didn't know how long it would take him to get back to normal after this.

"Miss me?" a dark figure popped up from behind his seat.

"*Bree!*"

He leaped out of the car and yanked open the door, pulling her out as if the vehicle had caught fire. He hugged her until she could not breathe, then smothered her face with kisses until she was breathless again.

"Oh my goodness," she managed. "I guess I should've called first."

"I love you, Bree," he held her face in his hands, gazing into her eyes intently. "I never got to tell you, I didn't want to scare you away. I didn't dare take a chance of losing you."

"Well, gosh, Hoyt, I love you too," she managed a chuckle, grabbing his hands gently so she could compose herself. "The Lord saved my life that night, He made me go tinkle so I was out of bed when that bomb went off. I thought of calling you, but then I thought if I went hiding, everyone'd think I was dead and that big dumb ox Reaper would go on about his business. Wait until I get my hands on him. First he throws me out a window, then he blows up my house."

"No, Bree, you're out of the game," Hoyt insisted. "I'm taking you to a hotel somewhere out of town, maybe Jersey or Pennsylvania. We can still have you play dead, but I will *never ever* let you risk your life like that again."

"I thought you said you loved me," she lowered her eyes.

"What?" he said incredulously, taking her face in his hands again. "I love you more than anything else in this world!"

"Well, then, don't try and stop me from finishing what I started," she said plaintively. "Six of his people are in jail, there's just him and those two tomboys that blew up my house. Plus I caught the rat he had in my office. I found out what he's planning, and I know how to catch him. Plus I know how to beat him. He drops his right when he throws his left jab."

"Whoa, hold on," he shook his finger in his ear. "I'm not hearing right. Did that bomb go off near your head?"

"He's got the formula and the ingredients for Kolokol-1," she explained. "It's a fentanyl-based morphine derivative that's aerosolized for quick dispersal. They used it at that Moscow theatre on the Chechen terrorists a few years back. It's not lethal unless it's absorbed in high doses, so the worst effect is going to be on the people directly beneath the point of detonation. If we can keep him from setting the bomb off at close range, all he's going to do is have a bunch of people walking around stoned on dope."

"Okay, you said we," he exhaled resignedly. "What's your plan, you crazy nut?"

"All right, I'll tell you, but you have to keep it a secret and you have to keep pretending I'm dead."

Pastor Mitchell had been grieved by the news of Sabrina's death, and he and the congregation held an impromptu prayer meeting that evening. He stayed behind to finish up some paperwork, preparing to meet tomorrow morning with the sponsors of the women's shelter that the proceeds from the barbecue fundraiser had made possible. He felt terribly guilty about having agreed to reschedule the picnic at her home, but had no way of knowing that such a thing could have happened. Many prayers were given up that evening for the sodomites who plotted Sabrina's death, and they begged the Lord to bring light into their lives and save their souls.

He heard a noise at the front door and could not help but feel a tinge of apprehension. He hoped it was one of the women having come back for something they might have left behind. He worried that it might have been one of the gay militants, not out of fear for his safety, but over the danger of the flock being unattended at such an important time in getting the shelter and adoption program underway.

"*Bree!*"

Sabrina scampered down the aisle and ran into his arms as Hoyt stood by the entrance, smiling approvingly. They hugged each other happily before he released her, wiping a tear of gladness from his eye.

"Oh, for heaven's sake, I thought we lost you for good," he said joyously, then did a double-take at her uniform. "Now, you're not planning on going out again, are you?"

"I think I'm gonna have to," she said quietly, then turned towards Hoyt. "You remember my boyfriend from the picnic. He's coming with me to make sure I come back in one piece."

"Aren't you a cop?" the Pastor asked. "Can't you report this and let the authorities handle this? Surely our entire law enforcement system can do more that this one girl."

"She told me she told you about this whole scheme of hers," Hoyt shook his head. "I know you've tried to talk her out of it before. You must know by now that pretty little head is filled with concrete."

"Sir, I think this goes far beyond whether she wants to bring the authorities in on this," Mitchell objected. "The band of killers she's after have threatened the lives of thousands of people!"

"There's a warrant out for the arrest of the Nightcrawler," he exhaled, pulling out a business card and setting it on the table in front of the pulpit behind Mitchell. "Besides, they'd probably send her to a mental hospital. I know they'll take my badge and throw me off the force for not turning her in. You can call that number if you like, kill two birds with one stone."

The Pastor took the card off the table after the couple left, staring at the door long after they had gone. He crumpled it in both hands, then went to his knees and began praying for the lives and safety of Sabrina Brooks and Hoyt Wexford.

New York City had one of the biggest Fourth of July extravaganzas in the country. They had scheduled an air show which featured vintage World War I aircraft, followed by a fly-by of jet fighters and transport planes from an aircraft carrier en route to the Middle East from the New York harbor. They would then have a large number of dirigibles, blimps and airships sailing across the River before the big fireworks show at nine PM.

The Octagon had rented out an offshore platform along the Hudson River not far from the Hudson Yards where they would put their plan into effect. Their blimp had a Happy Fourth of July slogan painted red, white and blue on its underside. The blimp was filled with a mixture of Kokolol-1 and helium the night before, and the air bags were inflated just before takeoff that morning. The Russian mobsters that serviced the blimp made the final ballast adjustments and it finally left the ground shortly before noon.

They reached one thousand five hundred feet, and began a slow circle around Manhattan Island to join the queue that would sail in procession over the East River near the Brooklyn Bridge at three PM. Beginning at the North Bronx, it was planned so that residents all over Manhattan would be able to see the flotilla. The show would last for three hours, giving people time to have dinner before settling back for the nine o'clock fireworks display.

The Octagon had rigged the gondola with explosives which could be detonated by a remote control device held by the Reaper. He and the others had scuba diving gear which they would put on as they came to the East River. They would dive from the gondola as the blimp descended from its original altitude, putting it at a proximity to the crowds in attendance where the explosion would do most damage. The resulting chaos would be such that no one would concern themselves with the divers as they made their getaway beneath the piers along the riverside.

"Just think, after this magnificent flight and an exciting swim across the East River, we will be on a flight to Paris this evening," the Reaper chortled as he looked out the gondola window at the swarms of humanity lining the parks and piers along the river. "The people down there also seem to be having a wonderful time. They'll be able to tell their grandchildren about this historic event. Too bad the people at the South Street Seaport and the Brooklyn Promenade will not be as fortunate."

"I just want this to be over," Callen Marlowe lit a cigarette as she gazed out at the sailboats cruising down the river towards the Seaport. "They're getting too damn close. I can't believe they found out about Rick. I think there's something he's not telling us. Besides, we're sitting ducks up here in this damned balloon. We're flying right into an air zone where they've got warplanes on exhibition."

"Just think of it as the biggest blow struck for gay rights in the history of mankind," Sheryl Harrington managed a chuckle. "I just wish I could see the looks on the faces of those haters when this thing blows up. Talk about fireworks, this is gonna be the LGBT's version of the Big Bang."

"Let's remained focused," Dalibor Branko said gently but firmly. His stomach churned with revulsion over the notion that he might somehow be linked with these perverts as a gay militant in the annals of history. "Once we come within two hundred yards of the Seaport, we will put on our air tanks and prime the explosives. We will begin losing altitude about one minute before the bombs go off, and we will dive into the water ten seconds before detonation."

At once they heard the sound of approaching helicopter blades, and they were startled as it grew loud enough to seem as if colliding with the blimp. They rushed to the windows of the gondola and realized that the chopper must have flown right over the blimp to have made such a noise.

"That idiot must have just got his license," Callen snapped angrily. "If he would've hit this thing with those helicopter blades, we would've had a tragedy here."

"Perhaps not so much for the people of New York as for us," the Reaper chuckled. He had been well known for standing unfazed on the battlefields of Serbia in the face of artillery bombardments.

The three mercenaries stared out at the bustling city below, each immersed in their own thoughts. The Reaper's mind was running in a different direction than his confederates'. Now that six of their number was in prison, they would be dividing the $100 million three ways. If he could figure out a way to eliminate these two transsexuals, he would be depositing a surreal amount of money into his own Swiss bank account.

Callen had already invested in a Spanish *hacienda* and had thought of going her own way once they reached Europe. At first her sex change operation had left her unfulfilled, and she even wondered whether she had made the right move. Yet there were many who told her she might be able to capitalize on having the best of both worlds. She had always been a strong, athletic man, but now enjoyed the look of a sexy, well-built woman. She had been approached by Arab nationals asking if she might be interested in working as an undercover operative, and she found the notion most intriguing. Though she eventually learned it was for an Al-Qaeda connected group, the figures they presented were too hard to turn down. She was introduced to the Reaper, and the meeting changed her life.

Dressed in her rubber scuba suit as were they all, she puffed reflectively on her cigarette as she wandered away from the control panel where the Reaper and the Scorpion stared expectantly at the south end of Manhattan about two miles away. All that was left was to make this dive and swim over to the Fulton Fish Market where their Russian connection was waiting with a bogus emergency truck. He would navigate through the chaos through the Wall Street area to the Staten Island Ferry terminal, where they would cross over and make a second connection. It would take them to JFK Airport, and quite possibly, out of the USA forever.

She heard an impact on the side of the gondola, and stared in amazement as a figure lowered itself from above and deftly climbed through an opened rear window. She remembered the figure from the incident in Garrison, the person who the Reaper had thrown out a second-story window. She remembered the face, the same face of the woman who they had assassinated with a bomb at her home just a couple of days ago. She could not believe that it was Sabrina Brooks, standing before her without her balaclava.

"You!" Callen managed as the Reaper and the Scorpion came up on either side of her.

"I suppose you have decided to leave your veil at home so it will be easier for the authorities to identify your body," the Reaper called out to her. The gondola was thirty feet in length, with plenty of space for passengers to move around in enjoying the unique experience.

"Well, at least you'll know for sure who it was that kicked your butt," Sabrina retorted, holding her gas gun in firing position.

"She can't get you both," the Reaper told his partners. "When I throw her out the window this time, I can assure you she will never be heard from again."

The Reaper had insisted that they not use handguns on their missions because it would be far easier for their lawyers to get them off the hook without them in case of arrest. Both the Tarantula and the Scorpion came up on either side of Sabrina, crouching as they prepared to rush at her. She feinted towards Callen, then turned and fired at Sheryl as the Scorpion charged at her. Sheryl choked and gagged, dropping backwards in a heap as she fought to catch her breath. Callen rushed Sabrina and was cracked across the jaw by the gas gun. Sabrina then dropped the weapon as she grabbed Callen's collar, slinging her over her outstretched leg. Callen tripped and was slung headfirst through an opened window and went flying out into the skies over Greenwich Village.

"Okay mister, game's over. Give me the detonator."

"Come on then, Miss Brooks. Why don't you take it off me?"

"With pleasure."

Sabrina moved towards him in a boxing stance, while the Reaper casually cocked his right fist while waving his left hand side to side towards her.

"You know, it's such a shame that we did not have the opportunity to join forces. That homosexual manager of yours, Rick Alfonso, gave us everything we wanted to know about your Company. That included your father's classified formulas for the WMD research. He's quite a wealthy man now, that pervert. We've paid him enough so that he should be able to start his own company about the size of your own."

"Yeah, well, you'll have the rest of your life to read about it in your padded cell. That is, if they don't take away your reading privileges."

The Reaper sprung like a cat, surprisingly nimble for a man of his size. He reached out to grab her as much as he got his range on her, then threw a murderous right cross.

Sabrina had a remarkable capacity for fearlessness. She would always credit her father for the way he had raised her, and her Heavenly Father for giving her the courage to face the unknown. Vern Brooks had enrolled her in swimming and ice skating classes as soon as she learned to walk, and got her into a rock climbing group when she was in grade school to help her overcome the natural fear of heights. He wanted his daughter to succeed in everything she put her mind to. He wanted to remove any obstacle to her success that might prevent her from realizing every dream.

Her biggest dream at this stage of the game was whipping the Reaper's butt for throwing her out a window and blowing up her bedroom. She had close to an eidetic memory and remembered how the Reaper had come at her last time. She dodged the right cross, bobbed underneath the outstretched arm and threw a left roundhouse kick at the side of his face. She did not make full impact but staggered him so he threw the left jab she was waiting for.

She knew that many boxers dropped their right hands ever so slightly when throwing the left jab. Her father, a lifelong boxing enthusiast, showed her the tapes of how Max Schmeling had spotted this in beating the legendary Joe Louis. She always looked for that, and spotted it when the Reaper beat her up before throwing her out the window. As the Reaper threw the left jab, she immediately sprang up with a second roundhouse kick. The steel toe of her left boot smashed directly into the man's temple, sending him sprawling backwards in a tangled heap.

"It's all over, Branko," she said as she saw the glassy look in his eyes. "Hand over the detonator and nobody gets hurt."

"I'm not going anywhere," the Reaper pulled the detonator from his pocket and showed it to her, a modified remote control device. "If I am captured, my enemies in Serbia would spare no expense in having me killed in prison."

With that, the Reaper pressed the red button on the device.

Chapter Ten

The Governor of New York met with the world press the next morning in a globally-televised news conference. The President of the United States had called him shortly after the aborted attempt to use a WMD on the crowds attending the Fourth of July celebration. The Coast Guard had recovered body parts along the East River amidst the debris from the gas-filled blimp that had exploded harmlessly above the harbor. DNA testing revealed that those killed in the blast were Dalibor Branko, Callen Marlowe and Sheryl Harrington.

Federal and State authorities announced that a call received by hero cop Hoyt Wexford confirmed that the victims of the blast were key members of the Octagon. Homeland Security had contacted INTERPOL, who verified that the DNA sampling matched that of Dalibor Branko. He was listed as missing in action at the end of the Serbian War, though INTERPOL had a warrant issued for his arrest in association with war crimes and crimes against humanity. Homeland Security said they would be wrapping up their investigation but considered the case closed.

"It is with great satisfaction that I am able to assure the people of the great State of New York that the threat posed by the terrorist organization known as the Octagon has ended. We have been informed by Homeland Security that these terrorists were working in conjunction with Al Qaeda, and the President of the United States has given me his personal assurance that no stone will be left unturned in uncovering these connections and bringing these criminals to justice."

"Numerous issues had arisen as to the status of the members of the Octagon that have been taken into custody. They have been identified as members of the LGBT community, and questions have been raised as to their civil rights having been violated during our investigations and law enforcement procedures. Let me assure everyone everywhere that the State of New York does not and will discriminate against any individuals regardless of race, creed, color or sexual orientation. By the same token, an attack on our citizens is an attack on the State itself. We will not hesitate to bring anyone to justice regardless of their orientation, and no one will be spared regardless of their status in our community."

"Finally, Officer Hoyt Wexford of the NYPD has testified as to the invaluable assistance in this case provided by the citizen known as the Nightcrawler. Although these are still unresolved issues related to the Nightcrawler in regard to this case, I hereby declare that all City and State charges and warrants against the Nightcrawler are being dropped. There are questions that have been raised that only the Nightcrawler can answer, and we ask that he step forward without fear of reprisal so that these matters may be addressed. In the meantime, on behalf of the people of New York, I express my gratitude to the Nightcrawler in helping end this terror threat."

Sabrina Brooks had been seen falling from the sky into the East River shortly before the explosion of the blimp occurring in the air space over Lower Manhattan. A group of people celebrating the holiday along the harbor managed to rescue her from the water. They recognized her from newspaper photos and assumed that she had been kidnapped by the Octagon but managed to escape. She begged them not to call the police, and instead they carried her to a nearby vehicle and brought her to Bellevue Hospital.

"Well, not that I enjoy seeing you in a hospital bed, but I can't help but think this'll keep you from doing any more Nightcrawling," Hoyt looked at her after the televised broadcast of the Governor's speech had ended. "At least for the time being."

"I think I've learned my lesson," Sabrina smiled reassuringly. "The doctor said I won't be able to walk without crutches for a while."

"That won't be a problem as far as you coming to my award ceremony on Saturday. I'm personally going to wheel you out there."

"You're sweet," she blew a kiss at him.

"Do that again," he said, hopping out of his chair and leaning over her. She kissed him on the lips, and they gazed lovingly into each other's eyes before he sat back down.

"Say, what's that thing by the pillow near your head?" he pointed.

"What's that?" she asked, reaching around so her hand touched against a small object. She picked it up and her eyes widened at the sight of a small velvet box. "Oh, Hoyt! I—"

"Not to worry, it's a friendship ring," he assured her. "I just thought I'd make it official. I want you to be my girl."

"So what did you think, Silly Billy, I *wasn't* your girl?" she said, slipping the ½ carat diamond ring on the platinum band onto her finger. "Ooh, how pretty!"

"Well, sweetheart, I've got a ton of paperwork waiting for me at Police Plaza thanks to that mysterious friend of yours," he got up again, coming over to kiss her before taking his leave. "I'll come back before closing if you're not asleep."

"Yeah, well, you better make sure they wake me up," she warned him.

The press was on hand when Pastor Mitchell arrived at the Christian Adoption Center on the Bowery that Friday morning. It had become a topic of discussion as the LGBT community continued to protest what they considered the Center's discriminatory practices. The Pastor took the opportunity to provide a definitive response on behalf of the Christian community.

"Christians recognize love as the greatest gift from God bestowed on humanity through our Lord Jesus Christ," the Pastor proclaimed as microphones were held towards him while cameras rolled. "The only distinction we make is between spiritual love and sexual desire. Although it is not ours to judge as to the nature of the love between individuals, platonic or otherwise, we do believe that the institution of marriage is the exclusive domain of a man and woman. This is not to deny the rights of any two individuals or an attempt to interpret or define their relationship. Our society has numerous legal recourses to protect the legal interests and social benefits of individuals, and we would fully support all efforts to further establish and define the rights of two people who have entered into a lifetime partnership, regardless of sexual orientation. We just ask that you respect the sanctity of marriage. Give unto Caesar that which is Caesar's, and give to God the things of God."

"We have also been asked to clarify our statements as respects our adoption policy. Once again, we do not question the rights of individuals or partnerships in our American society. However, as Christians, we contend that a child is God's gift to a man and a woman as a blessing of a natural family. Though we do not attempt to distinguish between relationships between two people, we would err on the side of caution where the well-being of a child is in question. If a relationship between two individuals is defined by its sexual orientation, then we believe that too many questions would be raised before entrusting the care and well-being of a child to persons in such an environment."

The interview went viral on the Internet, getting over a hundred thousand hits on You Tube. Christian activists around the world downloaded the clip, using it as an evangelical tool for their personal and Church ministries. It served to qualify the donations that were made by wealthy philanthropists, who were at first concerned over the LGBT backlash at the Church barbecue picnic. They were able to justify their gifts to the ministry by pointing out that the mission statement was a well-phrased credo rather than a reflection of right-wing conservative jargon and knee-jerk bias. Pastor Mitchell, as usual, downplayed the interview and gave the credit and the glory to the Lord Who gave him the words to speak.

Rita Hunt had taped the interview and played it back several times throughout the course of the day at the end of her first week at the Center. She received a modest salary as the manager for the facility, and had her hands full setting up an administrative system as best she could. She was satisfied with the fruits of her labor by the end of the afternoon, and yawned and stretched as she prepared to close it down for the weekend.

She had just logged off her PC when a young woman burst into her office and plopped down in the modest armchair before her desk. She threw her arms over the sides of the chair and kicked her feet out in front of her, dropping her head forward before wrinkling her brow at Rita.

"I think we've put this off long enough. Dinner's on me."

"Maybe if it falls in your lap," Rita grinned.

It was great to see Sabrina Brooks up and around again.

CPSIA information can be obtained
at www.ICGtesting.com
Printed in the USA
BVHW031440201020
591421BV00001B/42

9 781715 622510